Sultana's Dream
A Feminist Utopia

and Selections from
THE SECLUDED ONES

Rokeya Sakhawat Hossain. Reproduced by permission of Roushan Jahan.

Sultana's Dream
A Feminist Utopia

and Selections from
THE SECLUDED ONES

Rokeya Sakhawat Hossain

Edited and Translated by Roushan Jahan
Afterword by Hanna Papanek

The Feminist Press
at The City University of New York
New York

Dedicated to the inheritors of Rokeya's dream

"Sultana's Dream": Purdah Reversed, *"The Secluded Ones"*: Purdah Observed, and *Rokeya: An Introduction to Her Life* © 1988 by *Roushan Jahan*. Translation of selections from *The Secluded Ones* © 1981, 1988 by Roushan Jahan. *Caging The Lion: A Fable for Our Time* © 1988 by Hanna Papanek. "Sultana's Dream" and selections from *The Secluded Ones* are reprinted and translated, respectively, from *Rokeya Racanavali,* with the kind permission of the Bangla Academy, Dhaka, Bangladesh. All rights reserved.

Published by The Feminist Press at The City Uiversity of New York, 365 Fifth Avenue, New York, NY 10016

First edition, 1988
12 11 10 09 08 07 06 05 04   8 7 6

Library of Congress Cataloging-in-Publication Data

Rokeya, Begum.
    Sultana's dream and selections from The secluded ones.
    Bibliography: p.
    "Publications of Rokeya Sakhawat Hossain": p.
    1. Women—Bangladesh--Literary collections.
2. Purdah—Literary collections. 3. Rokeya, Begum.
4. Authors, Bengali—20th century—Biography.
5. Feminists—Bangladesh—Biography. I. Jahan,
Roushan. II. Papanek, Hanna. III. Rokeya, Begum.
Abarodha-b~sin. English. Selections. 1988. IV. Title.
PR9420.9.R65S86   1988   823   88-11033
ISBN 0-935312-98-6
ISBN 0-935312-83-8 (pbk.)

This publication is made possible, in part, by public funds from the New York State Council on the Arts. The Feminist Press is also grateful to Helene D. Goldfarb for her generosity.

Cover design: Lucinda Geist
The embroidery reproduced on the cover is from a work designed by Mrs. Surayia Rahman. It is reproduced with her kind permission.

Contents

Preface
Roushan Jahan and Hanna Papanek
vii

Chronology
xi

"Sultana's Dream": Purdah Reversed,
Roushan Jahan
1

Sultana's Dream
Rokeya Sakhawat Hossain
7

The Secluded Ones: Purdah Observed
Roushan Jahan
19

Selections from *The Secluded Ones*
Rokeya Sakhawat Hossain
24

Rokeya: An Introduction to Her Life
Roushan Jahan
37

Afterword
Caging the Lion: A Fable for Our Time
Hanna Papanek
58

Glossary
87

Publications of Rokeya Sakhawat Hossain
89

Preface

IN THIS BOOK, we look at purdah—the seclusion and segregation of women—through three pairs of eyes: those of an early twentieth-century Muslim writer who saw purdah from the inside and campaigned against it most of her life; those of a modern Bangladeshi literary scholar and feminist activist; and those of a modern North American feminist social scientist familiar with South Asia and purdah.

It is important to introduce Rokeya Sakhawat Hossain to a much wider readership—not only because her ideas are important but also because her short story "Sultana's Dream" is a feminist utopia that antedates by a decade the much better known feminist utopian novel *Herland* by Charlotte Perkins Gilman. By bringing this perceptive feminist foremother to the attention of a wider readership now, we hope to remedy a long period of neglect and make it clear that feminist sentiments grow from indigenous roots, without depending on foreign influence.

We see this book as being useful to three broad audiences. For those students and teachers interested in literature by and about women, here is a well-contextualized introduction to a little-known Asian author. For students and teachers of Asian studies outside Asia, here is an addition that focuses on women's experiences, which are all too often neglected. For Asian readers, here is an introduction to an Asian author who is not well known outside the language and culture of Bengal but whose experiences resonate for many South Asian readers.

For all three readerships, however, a sense of history is crucial, for purdah observance is not a uniform phenomenon either in space or time. Changes in political, economic, social, and cultural forces can affect women's lives with unexpected speed, and not always for the best. Rokeya's portrayal of women in purdah in *The Secluded Ones*, her collection of journalistic vignettes, must, therefore, be seen in terms of the rapid shifts over time that have affected purdah observance in South Asia and in view of profound differences not only between cultures but also, within the same society, between classes and regions. Ironically, the excesses of purdah observance described by Rokeya at the start of this century may seem unbelievable to some South Asian readers and all too imaginable to some others in places where purdah is on the rise.

"Sultana's Dream," a short story, and *The Secluded Ones*, factual reportage, represent two genres in which Rokeya worked and indicate her central focus on injustice against women. In "Sultana's Dream: Purdah Reversed," Roushan Jahan sets the scene for readers new to Rokeya, telling how Rokeya came to write the story and why it was written in English, and provides a literary analysis of the story. Similarly, in "*The Secluded Ones*: Purdah Observed," Jahan discusses the significance of these reports in the context of other writings of the time about purdah. In "Rokeya: An Introduction to her Life," Jahan provides a broader view of Rokeya's life, her other writings and ideas, and her activism. Finally, in her Afterword, "Caging the Lion: A Fable for Our Time," Hanna Papanek sketches aspects of purdah on a broad canvas, to show not only the diversity of practices called "purdah" but the decisive impact of purdah on outside observers of South Asia. Selections from Papanek's own observations of South Asian purdah include excerpts from the life history of a woman who left purdah reluctantly, under pressure from her husband. In the Afterword, Papanek also discusses some of the underlying forces—especially the social control of sexuality and reproduction—that affect the relations between women and men in societies where purdah exists.

This book should have been written sooner for we have both been concerned with its subject matter for a very long time. Other commitments—to our families and our other work—have made completion of the manuscript difficult. Our decision to finish it now is the the result of what we see as a rapid deterioration in the rights of women in many parts of the world, in many cultures, and many different religious traditions. Once again, women are being used as the targets of fears and resentments generated by rapid social change. Repressive regimes and powerful social movements in many parts of the world are once again tryng to restrict the human rights of women as part of their attempts to bring to their societies the imagined stability of a mythic past.

But our work has also benefited from what is part of the response to these attacks on the position of women: the rapid development of action and research on women's issues throughout South Asia, accompanied by a tangible growth of international feminist networks. We have both been active participants in these activities; in moments spared from research or conference work, we were able to exchange ideas about this book and, eventually, our draft manuscripts.

The book is also the product of a long friendship. In the twenty-five years we (and our families) have known each other and explored each other's countries, we have often talked about the joys and problems of being women in our very different societies. The question of purdah has never been far from our minds. Rokeya's story of reverse purdah became a part of our converstions after Roushan Jahan's sister, Rounaq Jahan, first told Hanna Papanek about this utopian story in the 1960s.

Over the years, we have accumulated too many debts to family, friends, and colleagues to recount them all and confine ourselves here to a list of more formal acknowledgements.

For comments on drafts of all or part of our essays, we thank Dr. Anisuzzaman, Professor, Department of Bengali, Dhaka University; Dr. Riffat Hassan, Professor and Chair, Religious Studies Program, University of Louisville; Dr. Malavika Karlekar, Centre for Women's Development Studies, New Delhi; and Dr. Bruce Pray, Department of South and Southeast Asian Studies, University of California, Berkeley.

For many reasons, we are deeply grateful to "Hamida Khala" and the members of her family who spoke so frankly about life in purdah. We also thank Ela Bhatt, General Secretary of the Self-Employed Women's Association, Ahmedabad, for sharing with us the story of the union organizer.

We are also grateful to the Bangla Academy in Dhaka for permission to publish "Sultana's Dream" and other excerpts

from *Rokeya Racanavali*, the collected works of Rokeya Sakhawat Hossain, which appeared under their sponsorship in 1973.
We also thank Women For Women, a research and study group
in Dhaka, under whose auspices Roushan Jahan published *Inside
Seclusion: The Avarodhbasini of Rokeya Sakhawat Hossain* (1981),
a translation of selected short essays by Rokeya.

Thanks are also due to Surayia Rahman, the Bangladeshi
artist who designed the embroidered quilt (*nakshi kantha*), a portion of which is reproduced on the cover, and to the anonymous Bangladeshi woman who stitched the entire embroidery.
Hanna Papanek, the owner of the embroidery, made the pho-
tographs used for the cover.

In the course of our individual work on purdah and Rokeya,
we have each been helped by the support of several institutions
that directly advanced our work on the present volume.
Roushan Jahan worked on her critical biography of Rokeya
while a Visiting Scholar at the Center for Asian Development
Studies, Boston University, with a grant from The Ford Foun-
dation (Dhaka). Hanna Papanek received support for research
and writing on sex segregation and female seclusion in South
Asia from the National Endowment for the Humanities.

Given the logistical difficulties of prolonged international
collaboration, we appreciate the support of the institutions that
make it possible by bringing colleagues together at intervals for
workshops and study tours. Most important in this connection
has been the sponsorship of the United Nations University (To-
kyo) of the Comparative Study of Women's Work and Family
Strategies in South and Southeast Asia in which we are both
active participants. Study grants from the Smithsonian Institution and the American Institute of Indian Studies for Hanna
Papanek's other research in India are also greatly appreciated.

Finally, we thank Florence Howe, Susannah Driver, and the
staff of The Feminist Press for their patient and helpful support
throughout the difficult process of getting a finished manuscript
from peripatetic authors living half a world apart.

Roushan Jahan, *Bangladesh*, and Hanna Papanek, *USA*

Chronology

1880	Rokeya is born in the village of Pairaband.
1896	Marriage to Khan Bahadur Syed Sakhawat Hossain, Deputy Magistrate, Bengal Civil Sevice. Settles in Bhagalpur, Bihar.
1903–4	First publication, of articles on the oppression of women, in various journals in Calcutta.
1909	Death of Khan Bahadur Syed Sakhawat Hossain in Calcutta, May 3. Rokeya establishes the Sakhawat Memorial Girls' School, Bhagalpur.
1910	Rokeya leaves Bhagalpur and settles in Calcutta.
1911	Rokeya reopens the Sakhawat Memorial Girls' School in Calcutta, March 16.
1916	Founds the Anjuman-e-Khawatin-e-Islam, Bangla (Bengali Muslim Women's Association).
1917	Inspection of the Sakhawat Memorial Girls' School by Lady Chelmsford, wife of the Governor General and Vicerory of India. Prominent figures such as the Agha Khan, Sir Abdur Rahim Moulana Mohammad Ali, and others help the school.

1926	Presides at the Bengal Women's Education Conference held in Calcutta.
1931	Address, "The Bengali Muslims on Their Way to Decline," given at the Sakhawat School.
1932	Rokeya presides at a session of the Indian Women's Conference held in Aligarh. Dies, December 9. Buried in Sodpur, near Calcutta. Condolence meeting attended by many Hindu and Muslim social workers and educators, both male and female, Albert Hall, Calcutta. Message of condolence sent by the Governor of Bengal. Condolence meeting held at the Sakhawat School. The *Monthly Mohammadi* brings out a special memorial issue.

"Sultana's Dream":
Purdah Reversed

Roushan Jahan

"SULTANA'S DREAM," published in 1905 in a Madras-based English periodical, *The Indian Ladies' Magazine*, is one of the earliest "self-consciously feminist"[1] utopian stories written in English by a woman. It is certainly the first such story to be written by an Indian woman. Its author, Begum Rokeya Sakhawat Hossain (1880–1932), is the first and foremost feminist of Bengali Muslim Society. One hesitates to use a term that is not context-free, and *feminism* does mean different things to different people, yet it is the term that automatically occurs to many who read Rokeya's work now. At the time she wrote this story, she had already attracted considerable attention as an essayist, having published several articles in Bangla dealing exclusively with the subordination and oppression of Bengali women, especially Bengali Muslim women.

Rokeya reminisced about writing this story in 1930, twenty-five years after its publication. As she remembered, she was all alone in her house because her husband, Khan Bahadur Syed Sakhawat Hossain, a Deputy Magistrate, was away on a tour of inspection. He was stationed in Bamka, a small town in the district of Bhagalpur, in the present-day Indian state of Bihar. The young Bengali Muslim woman must have felt especially lonely in a household where everybody spoke Urdu; for, although Rokeya spoke Urdu, Bengali was her native tongue. "To pass the time, I wrote the story."[2] Her motivation was partly to demonstrate her proficiency in English to her non-Bengali husband, who encouraged her to read and write English, and who was her immediate and appreciative audience.

1

Partly the desire must have been to test her ability in literary forms other than essays.

When Sakhawat returned, he did exactly what Rokeya had anticipated. He casually inquired about what she had been doing. "When I showed him the manuscript, he read the whole thing without even bothering to sit down. 'A terrible revenge!' he said when he was finished."[3] He was impressed with the story, which is not surprising, and sent it to his friend Mr. McPherson, the divisional commissioner of Bhagalpur, for comments. Like any other young author, Rokeya was immensely relieved to receive flattering comments from him. "In his letter to my husband he wrote, 'The ideas expressed in it are quite delightful and full of originality and they are written in perfect English. . . . I wonder if she has foretold here the manner in which we may be able to move about in the air at some future time. Her suggestions on this point are most ingenious.' "[4] On the basis of such remarks, Sakhawat persuaded her to send the story to *The Indian Ladies' Magazine*, which published it that year (1905). By 1908, Rokeya had gained enough confidence as an author to submit "Sultana's Dream" for publication as a book. It appeared that year from S. K. Lahiri and Company in Calcutta.

It is perhaps not surprising that most readers react to "Sultana's Dream" as a pleasant fantasy and not "a terrible revenge" on men for their oppression of women, as her perceptive husband did. Even those who did perceive the bitter truth under the sugar-coating seemed to welcome this after the tremendous anger and biting wit displayed without camouflage in her essays. Critics like Abul Hussain thought of similarities with Swift's *Gulliver's Travels*, a book Rokeya much enjoyed and to which she referred more than once in her essays. He thought that the extreme measure of secluding men in Ladyland was a "reaction to the prevailing oppression and vulnerability of our women. . . . perhaps Mrs. R. S. Hossain wrote this to create a sense of self-confidence among the very vulnerable Bengali women. . . . That women may possess faculties and talents equivalent to or greater than men—that they are capable of developing themselves to a stage where they may attain complete mastery over nature without any help from men and create a new world of perfect beauty, great wealth and goodness—this is what 'Sultana's Dream'

2

depicts. . . . I hope the male readers of 'Sultana's Dream' would try to motivate the women of their families toward self-realization."[5]

Indeed, to motivate Bengali Muslim women toward self-realization and to persuade their society not to obstruct their way to self-realization was the mission of Rokeya's life. "Sultana's Dream" was one of many sorties in her lifelong and relentless *jihad* (holy war) waged against some of the basic principles of her society. As a publicist in the cause of women, she wielded her pen with considerable skill. She had an unerring eye for the vulnerable points of the opponents. She also possessed a remarkable sense of the comic, which enhanced her resources as a challenger. Though her style is remarkably lively and witty (school children in Bangladesh are still grateful to her for not writing tremendously boring essays like many of her male contemporaries), she did not write primarily to entertain. Rather, she marshaled her thoughts and arguments in order to question the existing order of things, to raise doubts about seemingly accepted facts, and to motivate people to take the necessary actions to change customs she considered evil and unjust.

This mission may well account for the fact that Rokeya did not continue writing and publishing in English, despite flattering comments from her contemporaries about her use of that language. Her pen was, first, a weapon in her crusade for social reform. Since her main concern was to raise the consciousness of the men and women of her own class of Muslim Bengal, her own language was the most appropriate medium for achieving her purpose. Moreover, she was a careful stylist, keen to achieve the desired effect with the words she used. Let us not forget that English was the fifth language she learned. Perhaps she was not confident when using English. It is likely that her experiment with the language as a medium of her creative writing convinced her that the idiom of English was not suited to her particular gifts. Whatever the reason, and she never shed any light on it, we know that she used English only when compelled to do so.

"Sultana's Dream" is a utopian work, with strong satirical elements. The Indian context is unmistakable. For example, through the dialogue of Sultana and Sister Sara the untenability of many of the prevalent Indian notions of "masculine" and "feminine" character are demonstrated. Sultana extols the wonder of Ladyland and represents the Indian stereotype while Sister Sara presents the outsider's view. At the same time she is also the alter ego of the author. Through Sultana, Rokeya ridicules Indian stereotypes and customs.

Women in Ladyland are powerful, but to portray a society where women are in a position of power, Rokeya did not find it necessary to eliminate men or to propose anything so drastic as Charlotte Perkins Gilman did a few years later in *Herland*, in which parthenogenesis was the means for continuing a uni-sex society.[6] In Ladyland men are a part of the society but are shorn of power, as women were in Rokeya's India. They live in seclusion and look after the house and the children, again, just like the women in Rokeya's India. Women, the dominant group in Ladyland, do not consider men fit for any skilled work, much as Indian men thought of women at that time. It is as if the omnipotent author is punishing men in an ideal world, accord-ing to the laws of poetic justice, for their criminal oppression of women in the real world. Men are being paid in their own coin and with interest. Rokeya's story does not tell us whether Ladyland changes basic human nature. Perhaps that was not her intention. All we are certain of is that she never again suggested the extreme measure of male seclusion. Indeed, given Rokeya's yearning for liberty and equality, it is hardly likely that she would have found the domination of either sex agree-able.

Though the story is presented as a dream, an internal logic is maintained. Extraordinary things do happen but not by magic or through supernatural agencies. All is explained in terms of advanced technology. This technology serves human needs to beneficial ends. Here again the Indian context is very clear. Ladyland has many amenities that Rokeya's India lacked. We have only to think of the India of horse-drawn carriages, gas-lights, smelly, smoke-filled kitchens, dusty streets, natural dis-asters, famines and epidemics, cockroaches and mosquitoes—all the big problems and petty nuisances of Indian everyday life—to appreciate the utopian element and the trust the author has in the power of science and technology to solve these problems.

To us, living in the shadow of the nuclear threat, such faith and trust in the benevolent aspect of science and technology as that displayed by authors like Rokeya, or Gilman, may seem quaintly touching or slightly naive. But it would not have seemed so in the days before World War I.

Rokeya's emphasis on science and technology in Ladyland must also be seen in terms of the debate about women's education in her time and place. Among her contemporaries, even the most forward-looking Brahmos, who were generally in favor of education for women, emphasized a curriculum that was not strong in science and mathematics. In this context, Rokeya was not only stressing the need for female education in general but also a type of education that enabled women to excel in science.

Finally, a word about the style and language. By temperament an essayist, Rokeya rarely wrote fiction and rarely wrote in English. And yet, of course, "Sultana's Dream" is an extraordinary achievement, and one that is particularly enjoyable today. For readers in both the East and the West, the reversal of male and female in a simple and powerful plot is intellectually appealing as well as humorous. And today, when the empowerment of women and the need for a reappraisal of gender roles have become internationally prominent issues, Rokeya's story seems less utopian than it did in 1905.

A Note on the Text

The text of "Sultana's Dream" presented here is closely based on the text included in the collected works of Rokeya, *Rokeya Racanavali*, published in 1973 by the Bangla Academy of Dhaka. That text retains the style of Rokeya's early-twentieth-century Bangla-influenced English. For clarity to readers of this volume, capitalization, spelling, and punctuation have been standardized according to present-day U.S. conventions.

Notes to " 'Sultana's Dream': Purdah Reversed"

1. Ann J. Lane's introduction to Charlotte Perkins Gilman, *Herland* (New York: Pantheon Books, 1979, [1915]), p. xix.

2. Rokeya Sakhawat Hossain, "Bayujane Poncash Mile" ("Fifty

Miles in an Aeroplane''), in *Rokeya Racanavali* (Dhaka: Bangla Academy, 1973), p. 311. All translations of quotations from this volume are by Roushan Jahan from the original Bangla text.

3. Ibid.

4. Ibid.

5. Hossain, *Rokeya Racanavali*, pp. 601–2; quoted from the critical review by Abul Hussain, in the Bangla monthly magazine *Sadhana*, 1921.

6. Gilman, *Herland*.

Sultana's Dream

Rokeya Sakhawat Hossain

ONE EVENING I was lounging in an easy chair in my bedroom and thinking lazily of the condition of Indian womanhood. I am not sure whether I dozed off or not. But, as far as I remember, I was wide awake. I saw the moonlit sky sparkling with thousands of diamondlike stars, very distinctly.

All on a sudden a lady stood before me; how she came in, I do not know. I took her for my friend, Sister Sara.

"Good morning," said Sister Sara. I smiled inwardly as I knew it was not morning, but starry night. However, I replied to her, saying, "How do you do?"

"I am all right, thank you. Will you please come out and have a look at our garden?"

I looked again at the moon through the open window, and thought there was no harm in going out at that time. The menservants outside were fast asleep just then, and I could have a pleasant walk with Sister Sara.

I used to have my walks with Sister Sara, when we were at Darjeeling. Many a time did we walk hand in hand and talk lightheartedly in the botanical gardens there. I fancied Sister Sara had probably come to take me to some such garden, and I readily accepted her offer and went out with her.

When walking I found to my surprise that it was a fine morning. The town was fully awake and the streets alive with bustling crowds. I was feeling very shy, thinking I was walking in the street in broad daylight, but there was not a single man visible.

Some of the passersby made jokes at me. Though I could

not understand their language, yet I felt sure they were joking. I asked my friend, "What do they say?"

"The women say you look very mannish."

"Mannish?" said I. "What do they mean by that?"

"They mean that you are shy and timid like men."

"Shy and timid like men?" It was really a joke. I became very nervous when I found that my companion was not Sister Sara, but a stranger. Oh, what a fool had I been to mistake this lady for my dear old friend Sister Sara.

She felt my fingers tremble in her hand, as we were walking hand in hand.

"What is the matter, dear, dear?" she said affectionately.

"I feel somewhat awkward," I said, in a rather apologizing tone, "as being a purdahnishin woman I am not accustomed to walking about unveiled."

"You need not be afraid of coming across a man here. This is Ladyland, free from sin and harm. Virtue herself reigns here."

By and by I was enjoying the scenery. Really it was very grand. I mistook a patch of green grass for a velvet cushion. Feeling as if I were walking on a soft carpet, I looked down and found the path covered with moss and flowers.

"How nice it is," said I.

"Do you like it?" asked Sister Sara. (I continued calling her "Sister Sara," and she kept calling me by my name.)

"Yes, very much; but I do not like to tread on the tender and sweet flowers."

"Never mind, dear Sultana. Your treading will not harm them; they are street flowers."

"The whole place looks like a garden," said I admiringly. "You have arranged every plant so skillfully."

"Your Calcutta could become a nicer garden than this, if only your countrymen wanted to make it so."

"They would think it useless to give so much attention to horticulture, while they have so many other things to do."

"They could not find a better excuse," said she with [a] smile.

I became very curious to know where the men were. I met more than a hundred women while walking there, but not a single man.

"Where are the men?" I asked her.

"In their proper places, where they ought to be."

"Pray let me know what you mean by 'their proper places.' "

"Oh, I see my mistake, you cannot know our customs, as you were never here before. We shut our men indoors."

"Just as we are kept in the zenana?"

"Exactly so."

"How funny." I burst into a laugh. Sister Sara laughed too.

"But, dear Sultana, how unfair it is to shut in the harmless women and let loose the men."

"Why? It is not safe for us to come out of the zenana, as we are naturally weak."

"Yes, it is not safe so long as there are men about the streets, nor is it so when a wild animal enters a marketplace."

"Of course not."

"Suppose some lunatics escape from the asylum and begin to do all sorts of mischief to men, horses, and other creatures: in that case what will your countrymen do?"

"They will try to capture them and put them back into their asylum."

"Thank you! And you do not think it wise to keep sane people inside an asylum and let loose the insane?"

"Of course not!" said I, laughing lightly.

"As a matter of fact, in your country this very thing is done! Men, who do or at least are capable of doing no end of mischief, are let loose and the innocent women shut up in the zenana! How can you trust those untrained men out of doors?"

"We have no hand or voice in the management of our social affairs. In India man is lord and master. He has taken to himself all powers and privileges and shut up the women in the zenana."

"Why do you allow yourselves to be shut up?"

"Because it cannot be helped as they are stronger than women."

"A lion is stronger than a man, but it does not enable him to dominate the human race. You have neglected the duty you owe to yourselves, and you have lost your natural rights by shutting your eyes to your own interests."

"But my dear Sister Sara, if we do everything by ourselves, what will the men do then?"

"They should not do anything, excuse me; they are fit for nothing. Only catch them and put them into the zenana."

"But would it be very easy to catch and put them inside the four walls?" said I. "And even if this were done, would all their business—political and commercial—also go with them into the zenana?"

Sister Sara made no reply. She only smiled sweetly. Perhaps she thought it was useless to argue with one who was no better than a frog in a well.

By this time we reached Sister Sara's house. It was situated in a beautiful heart-shaped garden. It was a bungalow with a corrugated iron roof. It was cooler and nicer than any of our rich buildings. I cannot describe how neat and nicely furnished and how tastefully decorated it was.

We sat side by side. She brought out of the parlor a piece of embroidery work and began putting on a fresh design.

"Do you know knitting and needlework?"

"Yes: we have nothing else to do in our zenana."

"But we do not trust our zenana members with embroidery!" she said laughing, "as a man has not patience enough to pass thread through a needlehole even!"

"Have you done all this work yourself?" I asked her, pointing to the various pieces of embroidered teapoy cloths.

"Yes."

"How can you find time to do all these? You have to do the office work as well? Have you not?"

"Yes. I do not stick to the laboratory all day long. I finish my work in two hours."

"In two hours! How do you manage? In our land the officers, magistrates, for instance, work seven hours daily."

"I have seen some of them doing their work. Do you think they work all the seven hours?"

"Certainly they do!"

"No, dear Sultana, they do not. They dawdle away their time in smoking. Some smoke two or three choroots during the office time. They talk much about their work, but do little. Suppose one choroot takes half an hour to burn off, and a man smokes twelve choroots daily; then, you see, he wastes six hours every day in sheer smoking."

We talked on various subjects; and I learned that they were not subject to any kind of epidemic disease, nor did they suffer from mosquito bites as we do. I was very much astonished to hear that in Ladyland no one died in youth except by rare accident.

"Will you care to see our kitchen?" she asked me.

"With pleasure," said I, and we went to see it. Of course the men had been asked to clear off when I was going there. The kitchen was situated in a beautiful vegetable garden. Every creeper, every tomato plant, was itself an ornament. I found no smoke, nor any chimney either in the kitchen—it was clean and bright; the windows were decorated with flower garlands. There was no sign of coal or fire.

"How do you cook?" I asked.

"With solar heat," she said, at the same time showing me the pipe, through which passed the concentrated sunlight and heat. And she cooked something then and there to show me the process.

"How did you manage to gather and store up the sun heat?" I asked her in amazement.

"Let me tell you a little of our past history, then. Thirty years ago, when our present Queen was thirteen years old, she inherited the throne. She was Queen in name only, the Prime Minister really ruling the country.

"Our good Queen liked science very much. She circulated an order that all the women in her country should be educated. Accordingly a number of girls' schools were founded and supported by the Government. Education was spread far and wide among women. And early marriage also was stopped. No woman was to be allowed to marry before she was twenty-one. I must tell you that, before this change, we had been kept in strict purdah."

"How the tables are turned," I interposed with a laugh.

"But the seclusion is the same," she said. "In a few years we had separate universities, where no men were admitted.

"In the capital, where our Queen lives, there are two universities. One of these invented a wonderful balloon, to which they attached a number of pipes. By means of this captive balloon, which they managed to keep afloat above the cloudland, they could draw as much water from the atmosphere as they pleased. As the water was incessantly being drawn by the university people, no cloud gathered and the ingenious Lady Principal stopped rain and storms thereby."

11

"Really! Now I understand why there is no mud here!" said I. But I could not understand how it was possible to accumulate water in the pipes. She explained to me how it was done; but I was unable to understand her, as my scientific knowledge was very limited. However, she went on:

"When the other university came to know of this, they became exceedingly jealous and tried to do something more extraordinary still. They invented an instrument by which they could collect as much sun heat as they wanted. And they kept the heat stored up to be distributed among others as required.

"While the women were engaged in scientific researches, the men of this country were busy increasing their military power. When they came to know that the female universities were able to draw water from the atmosphere and collect heat from the sun, they only laughed at the members of the universities and called the whole thing 'a sentimental nightmare'!"

"Your achievements are very wonderful indeed! But tell me how you managed to put the men of your country into the zenana. Did you entrap them first?"

"No."

"It is not likely that they would surrender their free and open air life of their own accord and confine themselves within the four walls of the zenana! They must have been overpowered."

"Yes, they have been!"

"By whom?—by some lady warriors, I suppose?"

"No, not by arms."

"Yes, it cannot be so. Men's arms are stronger than women's. Then?"

"By brain."

"Even their brains are bigger and heavier than women's. Are they not?"

"Yes, but what of that? An elephant also has got a bigger and heavier brain than a man has. Yet man can enchain elephants and employ them, according to his own wishes."

"Well said, but tell me, please, how it all actually happened. I am dying to know it!"

"Women's brains are somewhat quicker than men's. Ten years ago, when the military officers called our scientific discoveries 'a sentimental nightmare,' some of the young ladies wanted to say something in reply to those remarks. But both the Lady

Principals restrained them and said they should reply not by word but by deed, if ever they got the opportunity. And they had not long to wait for that opportunity."

"How marvelous!" I heartily clapped my hands.

"And now the proud gentlemen are dreaming sentimental dreams themselves.

"Soon afterward certain persons came from a neighboring country and took shelter in ours. They were in trouble, having committed some political offense. The King, who cared more for power than for good government, asked our kindhearted Queen to hand them over to his officers. She refused, as it was against her principle to turn out refugees. For this refusal the king declared war against our country.

"Our military officers sprang to their feet at once and marched out to meet the enemy.

"The enemy, however, was too strong for them. Our soldiers fought bravely, no doubt. But in spite of all their bravery the foreign army advanced step by step to invade our country.

"Nearly all the men had gone out to fight; even a boy of sixteen was not left home. Most of our warriors were killed, the rest driven back, and the enemy came within twenty-five miles of the capital.

"A meeting of a number of wise ladies was held at the Queen's palace to advise [as] to what should be done to save the land.

"Some proposed to fight like soldiers; others objected and said that women were not trained to fight with swords and guns, nor were they accustomed to fighting with any weapons. A third party regretfully remarked that they were hopelessly weak of body.

"If you cannot save your country for lack of physical strength, said the Queen, try to do so by brain power.

"There was a dead silence for a few minutes. Her Royal Highness said again, 'I must commit suicide if the land and my honor are lost.'

"Then the Lady Principal of the second university (who had collected sun heat), who had been silently thinking during the consultation, remarked that they were all but lost; and there was little hope left for them. There was, however, one plan [that] she would like to try, and this would be her first and last effort; if she failed in this, there would be nothing left but to commit suicide. All present solemnly vowed that they would never allow themselves to be enslaved, no matter what happened.

"The Queen thanked them heartily, and asked the Lady Principal to try her plan.

"The Lady Principal rose again and said, 'Before we go out the men must enter the zenanas. I make this prayer for the sake of purdah.' 'Yes, of course,' replied Her Royal Highness.

"On the following day the Queen called upon all men to retire into zenanas for the sake of honor and liberty.

"Wounded and tired as they were, they took that order rather for a boon! They bowed low and entered the zenanas without uttering a single word of protest. They were sure that there was no hope for this country at all.

"Then the Lady Principal with her two thousand students marched to the battlefield, and arriving there directed all the rays of the concentrated sun light and heat toward the enemy.

"The heat and light were too much for them to bear. They all ran away panic-stricken, not knowing in their bewilderment how to counteract that scorching heat. When they fled away leaving their guns and other ammunitions of war, they were burned down by means of the same sun heat.

"Since then no one has tried to invade our country any more."

"And since then your countrymen never tried to come out of the zenana?"

"Yes, they wanted to be free. Some of the Police Commissioners and District Magistrates sent word to the Queen to the effect that the Military Officers certainly deserved to be imprisoned for their failure; but they [had] never neglected their duty and therefore they should not be punished, and they prayed to be restored to their respective offices.

"Her Royal Highness sent them a circular letter, intimating to them that if their services should ever be needed they would be sent for, and that in the meanwhile they should remain where they were.

"Now that they are accustomed to the purdah system and have ceased to grumble at their seclusion, we call the system *mardana* instead of zenana."

"But how do you manage," I asked Sister Sara, "to do without the police or magistrates in case of theft or murder?"

"Since the mardana system has been established, there has been no more crime or sin; therefore we do not require a policeman to find out a culprit, nor do we want a magistrate to try a criminal case."

"That is very good, indeed. I suppose if there were any dishonest person, you could very easily chastise her. As you gained a decisive victory without shedding a single drop of blood, you could drive off crime and criminals too without much difficulty!"

"Now, dear Sultana, will you sit here or come to my parlor?" she asked me.

"Your kitchen is not inferior to a queen's boudoir!" I replied with a pleasant smile, "but we must leave it now; for the gentlemen may be cursing me for keeping them away from their duties in the kitchen so long." We both laughed heartily.

"How my friends at home will be amused and amazed, when I go back and tell them that in the far-off Ladyland, ladies rule over the country and control all social matters, while gentlemen are kept in the mardanas to mind babies, to cook, and to do all sorts of domestic work; and that cooking is so easy a thing that it is simply a pleasure to cook!"

"Yes, tell them about all that you see here."

"Please let me know how you carry on land cultivation and how you plow the land and do other hard manual work."

"Our fields are tilled by means of electricity, which supplies motive power for other hard work as well, and we employ it for our aerial conveyances too. We have no railroad nor any paved streets here."

"Therefore neither street nor railway accidents occur here," said I. "Do not you ever suffer from want of rainwater?" I asked.

"Never since the 'water balloon' has been set up. You see the big balloon and pipes attached thereto. By their aid we can draw as much rainwater as we require. Nor do we ever suffer from flood or thunderstorms. We are all very busy making nature yield as much as she can. We do not find time to quarrel with one another as we never sit idle. Our noble Queen is exceedingly fond of botany; it is her ambition to convert the whole country into one grand garden."

15

"The idea is excellent. What is your chief food?"

"Fruits."

"How do you keep your country cool in hot weather? We regard the rainfall in summer as a blessing from heaven."

"When the heat becomes unbearable, we sprinkle the ground with plentiful showers drawn from the artificial fountains. And in cold weather we keep our rooms warm with sun heat."

She showed me her bathroom, the roof of which was removable. She could enjoy a shower [or] bath whenever she liked, by simply removing the roof (which was like the lid of a box) and turning on the tap of the shower pipe.

"You are a lucky people!" ejaculated I. "You know no want. What is your religion, may I ask?"

"Our religion is based on Love and Truth. It is our religious duty to love one another and to be absolutely truthful. If any person lies, she or he is . . ."

"Punished with death?"

"No, not with death. We do not take pleasure in killing a creature of God—especially a human being. The liar is asked to leave this land for good and never to come to it again."

"Is an offender never forgiven?"

"Yes, if that person repents sincerely."

"Are you not allowed to see any man, except your own relations?"

"No one except sacred relations."

"Our circle of sacred relations is very limited, even first cousins are not sacred."

"But ours is very large; a distant cousin is as sacred as a brother."

"That is very good. I see Purity itself reigns over your land. I should like to see the good Queen, who is so sagacious and farsighted and who has made all these rules."

"All right," said Sister Sara.

Then she screwed a couple of seats on to a square piece of plank. To this plank she attached two smooth and well-polished balls. When I asked her what the balls were for, she said they were hydrogen balls and they were used to overcome the force of gravity. The balls were of different capacities, to be used according to the different weights desired to be over-

16

come. She then fastened to the air-car two winglike blades, which, she said, were worked by electricity. After we were comfortably seated she touched a knob and the blades began to whirl, moving faster and faster every moment. At first we were raised to the height of about six or seven feet and then off we flew. And before I could realize that we had commenced moving, we reached the garden of the Queen.

My friend lowered the air-car by reversing the action of the machine, and when the car touched the ground the machine was stopped and we got out.

I had seen from the air-car the Queen walking on a garden path with her little daughter (who was four years old) and her maids of honor.

"Halloo! you here!" cried the Queen, addressing Sister Sara. I was introduced to Her Royal Highness and was received by her cordially without any ceremony.

I was very much delighted to make her acquaintance. In [the] course of the conversation I had with her, the Queen told me that she had no objection to permitting her subjects to trade with other countries. "But," she continued, "no trade was possible with countries where the women were kept in the zenanas and so unable to come and trade with us. Men, we find, are rather of lower morals and so we do not like dealing with them. We do not covet other people's land, we do not fight for a piece of diamond though it may be a thousandfold brighter than the Koh-i-Noor,* nor do we grudge a ruler his Peacock Throne.** We dive deep into the ocean of knowledge and try to find out the precious gems [that] Nature has kept in store for us. We enjoy Nature's gifts as much as we can."

---

*The Koh-i-Noor ("mountain of light") is the name of a large and exceptionally brilliant diamond in the possession of the Mughal rulers of India, currently part of the British Crown Jewels. To Indians, it is a symbol of great wealth.

**The Peacock Throne is a famous jewel-encrusted throne built for the Mughal Emperor Shah Jahan, also known for the Taj Mahal. It was carried away from Delhi by the Persian invader Nadir Shah. Its current location is the cause of much speculation. Many think that one of the thrones displayed in the Istanbul Museum is the Peacock Throne. It is a long-standing symbol of royal power and splendor to Indians.

After taking leave of the Queen, I visited the famous universities, and was shown over some of their factories, laboratories, and observatories.

After visiting the above places of interest, we got again into the air-car, but as soon as it began moving I somehow slipped down and the fall startled me out of my dream. And on opening my eyes, I found myself in my own bedroom still lounging in the easy chair!

The Secluded Ones: Purdah Observed

Roushan Jahan

I REMEMBER MY INTRODUCTION to *The Secluded Ones* clearly, like a vivid dream. I was playing with my younger sister while my mother was reading to her own sister. They seemed to be very absorbed in the book. I started to listen and presently found that the story was about a woman who wore something called a *burqa* (a kind of clothing I had never heard of) and who fell on a railway track. With mounting horror and disbelief I learned that her maid would not let anyone help her up, and finally she was run over by a train. My child's mind, reared on stories of miraculous rescues of persons in danger by heroes dashing in in the nick of time, found the grim ending totally unacceptable. "How could the stupid maid let the poor woman die like that? Why did the fools not do something to lift her up?" I burst forth, no longer able to contain my anger, which swiftly followed the first shock of horror. My mother, considerably startled, began to say something. But my sister, perceiving herself neglected, started crying. In the ensuing confusion, my queries got lost. Soon, the natural resilience of a child's mind prevailed and the gruesome story was put aside, apparently forgotten.

Years later, when I reread the story, the same thrill of horror and anger swept me, but this time pity was mingled in. Now, I was a child no longer. While I had never worn a burqa, I had seen people wearing them. I knew much more about purdah, the various ways of observing purdah, the need to maintain purdah—in short, all the things that a young woman growing up in Bangladesh (at that time, East Pakistan) needed to familiarize herself with. Though the severity of purdah practices ex-

19

perienced by Rokeya and her contemporaries can only be imagined by someone like me who is removed in time, the emotions that compelled her to write about the experience are bound to affect present-day readers very strongly. One is even thankful that though Rokeya herself described seclusion as "a silent killer like Carbon monoxide gas,"[1] she did not consent to rot in seclusion in silence. Like Dylan Thomas, who urged his dying parent to "rage against the dying of the light," Rokeya urged her sisters to rage and come out of darkness.

The Secluded Ones (Avarodhbasini in Bengali), a collection of forty-seven anecdotes documenting purdah customs (Muslim and Hindu) all over North India, was first serialized in 1929 in the well-known Bengali periodical the Monthly Mohammadi, and later collected and published as a book. It was the first book of its kind to be written in Bangla by a Bengali Muslim woman. There had been quite a few books and articles written in Bangla depicting life in the zenana (women's secluded quarters) in India. Recent scholarship has located some writings by Bengali Hindu women themselves, describing the suffocating conditions of their lives. But most of these are autobiographical in nature— journals, diaries, letters, and memoirs—and their tone is intensely personal.[2] Authors like Rabindranath Tagore (1861– 1941) and Sharat Chandra Chatterjee (1876–1938) had written about life in the zenana in many of their novels and short stories. Their scenes reflect great sensibility, keen observation, and even sympathy for women, but they are fragmentary and incidental to the plot. Rokeya's The Secluded Ones, on the other hand, is strictly nonfiction reportage; its purpose is to present authentic incidents highlighting the absurdity of the extreme seclusion imposed on the women of North India, particularly Bengali Muslim women.

The reports from The Secluded Ones reprinted here expose excesses of seclusion, presented sometimes with humor, sometimes with pain. They not only present the purdah customs then prevalent; they also show the attitude of the men and women of purdah-observing families. The attitude of non–purdah-observing persons toward purdah is also made clear. Above all, the attitude of Rokeya herself runs as a leitmotiv through these selections, and throughout the entire book. Rokeya did not pretend to be impartial. She selected incidents that exposed the ridiculous, the absurd, the horrible, and the tragic aspects of purdah observance. It is important to consider the historical context when reading these reports; they cannot be used to describe present reality.

The fact that purdah and status were closely connected is demonstrated by the fact that the maids in purdah-observing families were allowed a much greater mobility and visibility than their mistresses. The rules were flexible and could be bent to suit the needs of the elite. That the degree of purdah observance of their own women depended on the "purdahlessness" of another class of women did not seem to be paradoxical to the elites, both Muslim and Hindu, of the time. The significance of this paradox seems to have eluded the notice of Rokeya also. In this she was a child of her time and class.

The real value of *The Secluded Ones* lies in the fact that it shows that, in spite of everything, not all women submitted to purdah willingly or gladly. Many resisted, trying to assert their individuality. They even resented the fact that they had no control over their fates or lives. The rejection of strict seclusion by Rokeya herself shows that, no matter how strict, seclusion could not always smother a woman's quest for development and fulfillment.

It is in revealing this that *The Secluded Ones* differs from other accounts of Indian zenana life, particularly those written by foreign women, mostly British and American, who visited India in the late nineteenth and early twentieth centuries. Some foreigners, like Mary Frances Billington, were honest to detail, but they viewed the zenana life from a distance.[3] Their glimpses were necessarily brief and cursory. Even an Englishwoman who married an Indian Muslim, Mrs. Meer Hassan Ali, did not fully perceive the conflict women in purdah might feel. Even though she lived for many years as a member of an Indian household and made many visits to women in their zenanas, she felt that they were quite resigned to the restrictions of purdah.[4] Rokeya's accounts are fuller. Katherine Mayo's reaction to purdah, while as indignant as Rokeya's, was again quite limited.[5] Her prejudices were too strong; her pro-British and anti-Indian political views too pronounced.

Rokeya, on the other hand, had the advantage of belonging to the culture. Yet her exposure to Western culture through education and association gave her the necessary intellectual detachment to view purdah, particularly among Muslims, from a different perspective.

Rokeya's critical and derogatory presentation of purdah caused quite a stir in Bengal. Many readers, not familiar with purdah customs and the deliberate manipulation of religious laws, were shocked. Many conservative Muslims, on the other hand, were angry. Most Muslims, however, were embarrassed. Some even resented this revelation of what had so far been private. Magazines and periodicals, especially those run by the Muslims, like the *Mohammadi*, carried angry letters. She had previously been accused by Muslims of "whipping" her society and of lending credence to and being unduly influenced by the severely critical and condescending pamphlets issued by the Christian Tract society in Madras. As one irate critic put it, "to her everything Indian is bad and everything Euro-American is good."[6] The reports in *The Secluded Ones* were too unflattering and hard to accept. The Muslims, priding themselves on their comparatively liberal laws concerning the status of women, had so far been condescending to the Hindus. That there had been a real change in the situation and status of Hindu women wrought by the sociocultural reform movements of the nineteenth and early twentieth centuries, and that in the 1920s Hindu women were not as disadvantaged as they had been earlier, seemed to have escaped their notice. They seemed unaware of the gap between the status *de facto* and the status *de jure* of their own women. This inability to perceive the social realities was reflected in the fact that even the scathing remarks of Katherine Mayo did not upset them, for they felt that her barbs were marked for the Hindus only. Rokeya, however, was saying the same things about the Muslims. Her own unveiling of the hidden face of Mother India concerned the Muslims directly. A few of them tried to discredit Rokeya by treating *The Secluded Ones* as fictitious. In the words of one critic: "The readers would have been happy if the respected author had not presented us with these fictions and fables in the name of discrediting seclusion."[7]

Yet, within a short time, the detractors lost the battle. Rokeya's cause was upheld by younger, educated Muslims, both male and female. *The Secluded Ones* became a sourcebook to them while Rokeya became a source of inspiration.

A Note on the Text

This translation is based on the text included in *Rokeya Racanavali*. Many of the original terms have been retained. Consistency in transliteration is difficult, as words from more than one non-English language appear here. I have tried to use approximate orthographic transliterations wherever possible. Names of nineteenth- and twentieth-century persons and widely used non-English words (such as *purdah*) and place names are spelled according to conventions of anglicization.

Notes to The Secluded Ones: *Purdah Observed*

1. Rokeya Sakhawat Hossain, *Rokeya Racanavali* (Dhaka: Bangla Academy, 1973) p. 277. Quotation translated by Roushan Jahan.

2. For more information, see Chitra Deb, *Antahpurer Atma Katha (Life-Stories from the Inner Apartments)* (Calcutta: Ananda Publishers, 1984). Also Ghulam Murshid, *Reluctant Debutante: Response of Bengali Women to Modernization* (Rajshahi: Rajshahi University, 1983).

3. Mary Frances Billington, *Women in India* (London, 1895).

4. Mrs. Meer Hassan Ali, *Observations on the Mussulmauns of India: Descriptive of Their Manners, Customs, Habits and Religious Opinions, made during a Twelve Years' Residence in their immediate Society*, 2 vols. (London: Parbury, Allen and Co., 1832). Second ed., edited with notes and a biographical introduction by W. Crooke, appeared in 1917 and was reprinted in India (Delhi: Deep Publications, 1975).

5. Katherine Mayo, *Mother India* (New York: Harcourt Brace & Co., 1927).

6. *Navanur* 3, no. 5 (1905). Quoted in *Rokeya Racanavali*, p. 15.

7. *Monthly Mohammadi* (1931). Quoted in *Rokeya Racanavali*, p. 19.

Selections from
The Secluded Ones

Rokeya Sakhawat Hossain

Author's Introduction

FOR A LONG TIME, we have been used to seclusion. Therefore, we—especially I myself—had nothing in particular to say against seclusion. If one asks a fisherwoman, "Does rotten fish smell good or bad to you?" how would she answer that?

I am presenting the reports of a few incidents to my sisters for their reviewing—I hope they would find them interesting.

It is necessary to mention here that all over India seclusion is observed, not only against men but also against women "outside" one's own family. No woman, except the closest relations and housemaids, is allowed to see an unmarried girl.

Married women also hide themselves from gypsy women and such other professional itinerant performers and entertainers. Among women, whoever succeeds in hiding most in the corner like an owl proves thereby to be the most "aristocratic" by breeding.

Even wealthy urban women run away from the sight of English missionary women. Let alone English women, even the sight of Christian or Hindu women (though in saris but not veiled) would drive them to the safety of their locked bedrooms.

Report One

A long time ago, the daughters of the zemindar of Pairaband, a village in the district of Rangpur [Rokeya's natal village] were performing the ritual ablutions prior to the *zohr* [midday] prayers. All of them were through except "Miss A," who was in the middle of the ritual. Her personal maid, *Altar Ma*[1] was

24

pouring the water on her palms from a metal pitcher. Suddenly a tall and stout *Kabuli*[2] woman walked through the back entrance of the inner courtyard. Alas! What a stir! The water pitcher dropped from Altar Ma's inert fingers—she started screaming—"Alas! Where did this fellow come from?" The woman laughed and protested. "Fellow? Which fellow are you talking about? I am a woman." Miss A ran for her dear life and managed to reach her aunt's room. Out of breath, she tremblingly blurted out, "Aunty, a woman in trousers is here![3] The lady of the house was startled and asked, "Has she seen you?" Miss A, reduced to tears, nodded yes. The other women in the meantime stopped their prayers and rushed to shut all the doors to prevent the Kabuli woman from seeing the other girls of the family. From the speed and urgency with which they locked the doors one would have assumed that a wild tiger was loose in the courtyard.

Report Seven

Twenty-five years ago, a wedding was being solemnized in a Bengali zemindar's house. The house was full of guests. It was very late. Everyone in the house was sleeping except for a few burglars who planned to rob the house.

One of the burglars entered the house by digging a tunnel through the mud wall of one room. One of the night guards suspected something amiss and woke the head of the house. The zemindar and five of his brothers armed themselves quietly and started to look for the burglar. They were all upset and angry at the audacity of this burglar.

The thief, in the meantime, had entered one of the big bedrooms where several guests were sleeping. As soon as they saw a stranger entering the room, the women dived deep under the bedclothes and held their breath. The thief broke the wall safe and took everything he wanted. When he approached one Begum and asked for her jewelry, the rest of them hurriedly started taking off their jewelry to offer it quietly to the thief. The thief, noticing this, decided to wait patiently till this was accomplished. Unfortunately, there was a new bride in the group who, though able to take off her huge nose ring, was unable to take off her heavy earrings, all entangled in her hair. The thief, after a polite wait, became impatient. He took out his sharp knife and after severing the ears of the bride beat a hasty retreat.

While all these things were taking place inside this room, the men of the house, armed to the teeth, were looking about for the thief. The women did hear them moving around but none made a sound because then this thief, not of the "permitted category," would hear her voice. As soon as he was out of the room, they started screaming.

My dear sisters, this is how we honor our purdah customs!

Report Eight

Once, a house caught fire. The mistress of the house had the presence of mind to collect her jewelry in a handbag and hurry out of the bedroom. But at the door, she found the courtyard full of strangers fighting the fire. She could not come out in front of them. So she went back to her bedroom with the bag and hid under her bed. She burned to death but did not come out. Long live purdah!

Report Eleven

I went to Ara [a small town in Behar] in 1926. Two of my granddaughters (actually the daughters of my stepdaughter) were getting married. I went to attend their weddings. The pet names of the two girls were Mangu and Sabu. At that time they were confined in the Maiya Khana.[4] In Calcutta the bride-to-be usually stays only four or five days in such confinement. But in Behar the girls are kept in such solitary confinement for six or seven months.

I could not stay in Mangu's "cell" for long—I felt suffocated in that close room. I opened the window but within a couple of minutes a haughty Begum walked over and closed the window, remarking curtly, "The bride is in the draught." I had to leave the room. I failed to stay in Sabu's cell even for a minute. Those poor girls, at that time, had already stayed in those rooms for six months. Ultimately, Sabu had a spell of acute hysteria. This is how we are trained to endure seclusion.

Report Fourteen

The following incident happened about twenty-two years ago. An aunt, twice removed, of my husband, was going to Patna from Bhagalpor; she was accompanied by her maid only. At Kiul railway junction, they had to change trains. While boarding the train, my aunt-in-law stumbled against her voluminous burqa and fell on the railway track. Except her maid, there was no woman at the station. The railway porters rushed to help her up but the maid immediately stopped them by imploring in God's name not to touch her mistress. She tried to drag her mistress up by herself but was unable to do so. The train waited for only half an hour but no more.

The Begum's body was smashed—her burqa torn. A whole stationful of men witnessed this horrible accident—yet none of them was permitted to assist her. Finally her mangled body was taken to a luggage shed. Her maid wailed piteously. After eleven hours of unspeakable agony she died. What a gruesome way to die!

Report Seventeen

About fourteen years ago, we had a teacher from Lucknow [capital of old Oudh, an important city in modern Uttar Pradesh in India] in our school. Her name was Akhtar Jahan. At that time, her three daughters were studying in our school. One day she was commenting on the immodesty of modern girls, laying regretful emphasis on the shameless conduct of her own daughters.

Then she started to talk about her own youth and remembered an extraordinary thing that had happened shortly after her marriage. She related that she was married when she was only eleven. When she went to her father-in-law's house, a corner room was allotted to her. It was rather lonely and farther away from the rest of the house. A younger sister of her husband would come to her room three or four times a day to look after her needs, especially to accompany her to the toilet. One day, for some reason, the sister-in-law did not come for a long time. The poor bride needed to go to the toilet badly but could not. [A new bride does not wander about the house by herself; it is deemed highly improper.]

Now, the brides of Lucknow used to get *pan-dans* [betel-leaf containers] from their parents as part of their dowry and bride-gift.[5] One of her huge containers was in her bedroom. She emptied the container of all the betel nuts and spices; she tied all these in a handkerchief. What she then filled the container with is not fit to be written about. In the evening, when a maid from her father's house came to prepare the bed, the bride tearfully told the maid how she had abused the container.[6] The maid took it from under the bed and consoled her, "Please don't take on so. I'll see to it that this is tinned again. Let the betel nuts stay in the handkerchief for now."

Report Eighteen

A doctor from Lahore has thus described his experience of purdah—

Whenever he went to visit a patient in a purdah house, he would find two maidservants holding a thick blanket in front of the bed. He would put his hand below the blanket and extend it to the other side of the blanket. The patient would then put her wrist in his hand to enable him to take her pulse. (A certain non-purdah lady asked me once, "If there was no woman doctor available, how would you let a male doctor examine your tongue? You could not possibly make a hole in the blanket and protrude your tongue through that hole?" I am presenting [this] question to my sisters with one of my own in the hope of finding an answer. How would they let doctors examine their eyes, teeth, and ears?)

[The doctor told me:] "A certain Begum was down with pneumonia. I said, "the condition of the lungs will have to be examined. I could examine it from the back." The nawab [head of the family] ordered, "Ask the maid to put the stethoscope wherever necessary." Of course, it is common knowledge that the stethoscope has to be shifted in various positions before any diagnosis is possible. Yet I had to comply with the nawab's commands. The maid took the end of the stethoscope inside the blanket and put it in place. After a few minutes I was getting really worried at not hearing any sound. For once, I decided to be audacious and lifted the corner of the blanket nearest me. To my consternation and disgust, I found the stethoscope resting on the Begum's waist. I was so irritated that I left the room immediately. The nawab Sahib had the gall to ask me what I made of the case! What the —, did he expect me to be omniscient?''

Report Twenty-three

Let us leave the experiences of other people. Let me share with you some of my own experience of purdah. Ever since I turned five, I have had to hide myself from women even. I could not understand the rationale behind it. Yet I had to disappear as soon as strangers approached. Men, naturally, were not allowed in the inner apartments. Therefore, I did not suffer from them. But women were permitted to roam around the inner apartments quite freely, and I had to hide from them. The village women dropped in for sudden visits. Somebody would make a sign and I had to find the nearest hiding place—the kitchen; inside the rolled mats of the maids; under the beds even.

I had to run for a hiding place just like little chicks who run to their mother whenever the hen flashes a sign warning them of approaching kites or hawks. But there was a difference. The little chicks had a foreordained place—their mother's wings— where they could hide. But I had no such naturally determined, safe hiding place. Moreover, the chicks instinctively recognize the danger signals sent by the mother hen. I, alas, had no such instinctive understanding. Therefore, at times, I would fail to interpret signals correctly and be slow in hiding. At such times, the well-wishing female elders of the family never hesitated to berate the "shameless and immodest conduct of modern hussies" like me.

When I was five, we stayed in Calcutta for a while. Once, the aunt of my second sister-in-law [wife of second older brother] sent two maidservants to visit with her. They had a "free pass" to wander the length of the house—and I had to run like a deer fleeing the hunters in all sorts of hiding places, behind doors and under tables. They usual hiding place was the attic on the third floor which was seldom frequented by the family. My ayah would carry me there in the morning and I would stay there the whole day. When the two maids finished surveying the rest of the house, they decided to look at the attic. My nephew [older sister's son] Halu, who was also five, ran to warn me of the impending catastrophe. Fortunately for me, the room had an old four-poster. I crawled under it, hardly daring to breathe—lest those heartless women hear the sound and look under the bed. There were a few empty boxes and old stools stored in the room. Poor Halu summoned all the strength of his five-year-old body and managed to drag a few of them near me. We arranged them around me to afford better cover. No one, except Halu, came to ask me whether I needed anything. He would bring me some snacks or a glass of water when asked to do so. Sometimes, though, he would go down to fetch something and would not come back for a long time. He was only a boy of five, after all, and easily got involved in games. I had to stay in this miserable plight for four days.

Report Twenty-five

In the eleventh report of this book, I mentioned that I went to Ara in 1924 to attend the wedding of my granddaughters. But while there, I saw nothing of the town except the house and the sky above. When I talked to my "daughter" (actually she was the girl whom my stepson-in-law married after the death of his first wife, my stepdaughter) she pleaded with me thus, "Please mother, would you ask your son-in-law to show you the town? Then we would also be able to see a little of this place. I have been living here for the last seven years but I have seen nothing." The newly wedded girls, Mangu and Sabu, also chorused earnestly, "Yes, oh yes! Please, Granny! If you'd only ask my father."

I asked my son-in-law to hire a coach for us so that we might ride around the town. For several days, he politely informed me that he had not been able to find a suitable carriage for us. Finally, one afternoon, his son (a boy of eleven) ran in to inform us that a hired carriage had arrived but a slat in the window was broken. Mangu implored, "Oh, please, don't let them send this away. We could cover that window carefully—couldn't we?" Sabu whispered, "Oh, good! We would be able to see better through that hole in the window!" We were ready, but whenever we asked about coming out we were advised to wait. The carriage was not curtained properly.

When we finally came out I found (Allah be praised) that the carriage had been completely covered by three heavy Bombay silk saris. The door of the carriage was opened and closed by my son-in-law, who tied the sari ends securely with his own hands. After a while, Mangu taunted Sabu, "Well, where is that hole through which we were going to see things so well?" After a while, the girls did discover a tiny tear in the sari cover. Mangu, Sabu, and their stepmother eagerly took turns peering through that little tear. I just could not bring myself to compete with them.

Report Twenty-nine

I attended a Ladies' Conference held in Aligarh. Many of the delegates had various types of burqa on. One had a strange burqa on. I mentioned this and she immediately said, "Oh, no! Don't talk about burqa. I had such horrid experiences." She related a few of those experiences.

Once she went to attend a wedding ceremony in a Bengali Hindu family. As soon as the children saw her coming in a burqa, they started screaming in fright and began to hide. Her husband has some other Bengali Hindu friends. She was obliged to pay at least one visit to each of them. But she created panic in every house. The children started trembling and screaming at the sight of burqa.

Once she came to Calcutta. In the evening she and her companions, all burqa-clad, went out in an open-top car. The children along the way started shouting, "Oh, my God! What are those?" One of them screamed, "Quiet, everybody! I'm sure those are ghosts." When the front part of their burqa moved in the breeze, someone said, "Hey, look, the ghosts are moving their trunks like elephants. Run, run! They are after us!"

Once she went to Durjeeling. At Ghum station, a crowd was observing a midget. He was only as tall as a boy of seven or eight, but he had the face of an adult, with a full beard and all. Suddenly she found that the curious eyes of the crowd were turned upon her. They were not amused by the midget anymore. Her burqa was infinitely more entertaining!

When they reached Durjeeling, they decided to go out after

dinner. They took a rickshaw to the Mall. The Mall was crowded. People were watching the soldiers returning from Tibet that afternoon. Her rickshaw-bearer parked the rickshaw on a side and joined the crowd. After a while she found the pedestrians taking a look inside her rickshaw.

Whenever she went for a walk, the dogs started howling and followed her. A horse or two reared when confronted with her. Once while she was visiting a tea garden, a little Gurkha girl raised a pebble to hit her.

Once she was walking with four or five other burqa-clad women. While walking near a little stream, all of them stumbled in the pebbles and mud and fell down. The workers in the tea garden nearby ran and rescued them. One of them chuckled and said affectionately, "Look at you! You have shoes on and that sack. Of course, you'd fallen in the stream. What else can you expect?" Alas, the embroidered veils of the Begums were soiled. Their burqas were soaked!

On top of all this, whenever they walked, they would hear mothers trying to hush their crying babies, pointing to them and saying, "Hush, child, hush. Look, those are Mecca and Medinah. See, those hooded witches—they are Mecca and Medina."

Report Thirty-seven

A train was coming from the western provinces of India to Calcutta. In the station of Bali, three burqa-clad women boarded the "female" compartment. There were a lot of Muslim women in that compartment. They thought it curious that even after the train left the station, these three women did not raise their *nekab* [the detachable front part of the burqa covering the face]. Suddenly they became rather suspicious. Also, the height of these newcomers was rather awe-inspiring. After they had prayed silently for a few moments, the train stopped at Lilua station. A women ticket-collector got into their compartment. Immediately one women complained about those three women. Before the ticket-collector could advance toward them, the one next to the door on the opposite platform jumped down and ran away. The ticket-collector shouted, "police,

police," and caught hold of one. When the *nekab* was raised, a face full of mustache and beard was revealed. The ticket-collector, stunned, could only mutter—"What, beard and mustache in a burqa?"

Report Thirty-eight

A certain lady doctor, Miss Sharat Kumari Mitra [Hindu], whom I know rather well, was telling me the other day, "If you only knew the trouble some of you Muslim women cause me. Even the smallest timely assistance is out of the question. No matter what it is—a clean bandage or hot water—one has to wait so long for it."

Once a servant from a distant village came to ask her to go and see the younger Begum of the house. She had a severe toothache, the servant informed the doctor. The doctor took the medicine and instruments necessary for extraction of teeth. After she reached there she found that the younger Begum was actually suffering labor pain—not toothache! What was the doctor to do? She was now in Jamgaon, which is eight miles away from Bhagalpur where she lived. She could not possibly take the same pair of horses back to Bhagalpur because the pair was already exhausted. But Jamgaon was like a village. Horse-drawn carriages or palanquins were rarely to be found.

Somehow she managed to get back to Bhagalpur and procure the medicines and instruments necessary for delivering a child. By the time she returned to Jamgaon, the poor patient was in a critical condition. When Dr. Mitra asked for an explanation from the mistress of the house as to why she was so misinformed about the problem, the senior Begum answered, "I had to send a man to you; what could I talk about but toothache? How could I have told a man about the real situation? Wouldn't that have been too embarrassing for both of us? What sort of a lady doctor are you if you don't have the sense to realize that?"

Report Forty-seven

In the words of a poet:

> Not fiction, not poetry, this is life.
> No theatre this, but my real house.

Only three years ago, we had our school bus. The day before the bus came, one of our teachers, an English woman, had gone to the auto depot to inspect the bus. Her comment was, "This bus is horribly dark inside. Oh, no! I'll never ride that bus!" When the bus arrived, it was found that there was a narrow lattice on top of the back door and the front door. Excepting these two pieces of latticework, three inches wide and eighteen inches long, the bus could be called completely "airtight"!

The bus took the girls to their homes that first afternoon. The maid, accompanying the girls, reported after she came back that it was terribly hot inside the bus. The girls were very uncomfortable. Some of them vomited. Some of the little girls were whimpering in the dark.

Before the bus went to fetch the girls on the next day, the English woman who taught in our school opened the shutter of the back door. She hung colored curtains on the open shutters. Even then it was found that a few of the girls fainted away, a few of them vomited on the way, and most of them had headaches, etc. In the afternoon, the aforementioned teacher opened the shutters on the side of the bus and hung curtains there also.

That evening, a Hindu friend, Mrs. Mukherjee, came to see me. She was glad to know about the progress the school was making. Suddenly she said, "Incidentally, what a fine bus you have! The first time I saw it, I thought a huge chest was being drawn on wheels. My nephew ran out and said, "Oh, aunty! Look! The moving black hole of Calcutta is passing by! Really! How can the girls possibly ride that bus?"

On the afternoon of the third day, several of the mothers came to complain. They said, "Your bus is certainly God's punishment. You are burying the girls alive!" I said, helplessly, "What can I do? If the bus was not such, you would have been the ones to criticize the bus as "purdahless." They said angrily, "What? Do you want to maintain purdah at the expense of our children's lives? We are not going to send our daughters to your school anymore!" That evening the maid reported that every guardian complained about the bus and warned that the girls would not ride this sort of bus.

The next evening, I had four letters. The writer of the letter written in English had signed himself, "Brother-in-Islam." The other three were in Urdu. Two of these letters were anonymous.

The third one had five signatures. The import of all four letters was the same—all of them were from well-wishers. For the continuing welfare of my school they were informing me that the two curtains hanging by the side of the bus moved in the breeze and made the bus purdahless. If something better was not arranged by tomorrow, they would be compelled, for the benefit of the school, to write in the various Urdu newspapers about this purdahlessness and would stop the girls from riding in such a purdahless bus.

What a dilemma I was in—

If I don't catch the cobra
The King will have my head—
If caught carelessly
Surely the cobra'd bite me!

I do not think anyone else had tried to catch such a cobra [the irate critics] to satisfy the whims of such a king [the equally irate guardians]. On behalf of the women imprisoned in seclusion, I wish to say—

Oh, why did I come to this miserable world,
Why was I born in a purdah country!

Notes to Selections from The Secluded Ones

1. Mother of Alta; in Bangladesh rural adult women are customarily addressed as "Mother of so-and-so" or "Wife of so-and-so" by persons not related to them by blood or marriage.

2. Kabuli is someone who hails from Kabul in particular or from Afghanistan or Northwest Frontier province by extension. In the British period, quite a few Afghan moneylenders and businessmen frequented the eastern provinces of India.

3. The women of Afghanistan and the Muslim women of northwest India dress in trousers, which may be quite loose-fitting or tight-fitting, and a tunic generally reaching their knees.

4. The bride-to-be used to be confined in a close room after the turmeric-paste ceremony which followed the formal engagement. The groom's family sent new clothes and turmeric paste which was smeared on the face and hands of the bride. This seems to be more strictly followed outside Bengal.

5. Pan-dans were made of various metals and came in various sizes.

The offering of *pan*, or betel leaf, with various *masala*, or spices, to guests was as much a part of Lucknow etiquette as the tea ceremony was to the Japanese.

6. It is customary for the parents of a bride to send a maid from the house to look after the girl's needs and also to put her clothes and other belongings in order when she goes to her in-laws' house for the first formal stay.

Rokeya:
An Introduction to Her Life

Roushan Jahan

Rokeya Sakhawat Hossain was born in 1880 in Pairaband, a
small village in the district of Rangpur in the north of present-
day Bangladesh, at the time of her birth a part of the colonial
British province of Bengal Presidency. Her date of birth is un-
certain, which is not surprising in a region which even today
lacks a well-regulated system of registering births and deaths.
Though some maintain that she was born on December 9, 1880,
citing her nephew as the source, this date is open to doubt.

Of her parents, Rokeya says little beyond, "I never knew
what parental love was."[1] Her mother, Rahatunnessa Sabera
Chowdhurani, remains a shadowy figure. She was the first of
four women her husband married. One of her co-wives was said
to have been European.[2] Rohatunnessa gave birth to two sons
and three daughters. Her rigid conformity to purdah observance
was the only memory of her that Rokeya recorded, in the dedication to *The Secluded Ones*, the only book she dedicated to
her mother.[3]

Rokeya's father, Zahiruddin Mohammad Abu Ali Saber, was
an extravagant and extremely conservative zemindar (large
landholder) whose rambling estate was a stronghold of the traditional way of life. He was said to have learned seven lan-
guages: Arabic, Persian, Urdu, Pushto, English, Hindi, and
Bangla.[4] His children seem to have inherited his linguistic ap-
titude. Like other upper-class Muslim men of his time, he encouraged his sons to learn Arabic, Persian, and Urdu. The use
of Bangla was frowned upon by many upper-class Muslims because it was also the native tongue of non-Muslims. Conscious
of the growing prestige and advantages a modern education

could bestow on young men (especially attractive was the pros-
pect of joining the government service), however, he allowed
his two sons, Abul Asad Ibrahim Saber and Khalilur Rahman
Abu Jaigam Saber, to be taught Bangla and English at first at
a local school and then at the elitist St. Xavier's College in
Calcutta. Thus they could meet influential persons who might
facilitate their entry into the civil service.

But where the formal education of his daughters was concerned he displayed indifference. This was not, as we today may
hasten to assume, proof of any lack of parental love. The practice of the time was to teach Bengali Muslim girls of the upper
classes only to recite the Quran (often without any explanation
of the text) and in exceptional cases to read a few primers,
concerned mostly with ideal feminine conduct and written in
Urdu, the language of the Muslim elite in northern India. These
girls were not usually encouraged to read and write in Bangla.
Defying custom, and valuing their Bengali identity over their
religious one, Rokeya and her gifted elder sister, Karimunnessa,
persisted in learning Bangla. Karimunnessa used to squat in the
inner courtyard of their house and draw the Bangla alphabet
on the ground with a stick, under the supervision of her younger
brother, who was allowed to go to school and learn both Bangla
and English. Once, when she was deeply engrossed in reading
a Bangla *Puthi* (a popular tale written in verse), her father dis-
covered her. She nearly fainted in fear. Her father, sensing her
fear, did not forbid her outright to read Bangla books. The
malicious criticism of relatives, however, soon put a stop to it.
Karimunnessa was sent by her father to live in close confinement at Baliadi, the estate of her maternal grandparents, and
was married off before she was fifteen.[5] But Karimunnessa had
an insatiable thirst for knowledge and later encouraged Rokeya
to continue reading and writing Bangla. As Rokeya so hand-
somely acknowledged in the dedication to Part 2 of the *Motichur*, "That I had not forgotten Bangla during my long stay (14
years) in Bhagalpur, where there was none to speak Bangla, was
only due to you. It was your care and concern and encouragement that motivated me [to write in Bangla]."[6]

Throughout her life, Rokeya was haunted by the waste of
human potential that she saw in Karimunnessa's fate. It
strengthened her determination to fight against the blind ob-

servance of customs she considered absurd. In *The Secluded Ones*, Rokeya graphically describes the strict observance of purdah in her family and the way, from early childhood, she and her sisters had to hide not only from men but also from women who were outside their kinship network.

The support and encouragement Rokeya received from her eldest brother, Ibrahim Saber, prevented the destruction of her own potential, at least during her formative years. Ibrahim Saber had been exposed to Western thought and culture; he was strongly in favor of women's education. He taught Rokeya both Bangla and English. Rokeya's first biographer and close associate, Shamsunnahar Mahmud, revealed that, in order to avoid criticism and interference from parents and relatives, brother and sister had to wait for their tutorial session until everyone in the house, especially their father, had gone to sleep.[7] The love and deep gratitude that Rokeya felt for this brother fill the dedicatory paragraph of her only novel, *Padmaraga*: "You have moulded me from childhood . . . your love is sweeter than honey which after all has a bitter after-taste; it is pure and divine like Kausar [the stream of nectar flowing in heaven mentioned in the Quran]."[8]

Rokeya's exceptional luck in having relatives who were sympathetic and supportive also held true in her marriage. Her husband, Syed Sakhawat Hossain, a civil servant born in Bhagalpur (in the Bihar region of Bengal Presidency), was educated in Patna, Calcutta, and London. When Sakhawat was stationed at Rangpur, Rokeya's eldest brother, Ibrahim, met him and was very favorably impressed. Though Sakhawat was a widower and in his late thirties, Ibrahim persuaded his family to marry Rokeya to Sakhawat.[9] They were married in 1896 when Rokeya was only sixteen.[10]

Sakhawat was a man of liberal attitude who wanted from his wife not the traditional duty and obedience but love and sympathy; he not only loved her, he was also proud of her. They had two daughters, who both died in infancy; Sakhawat's deep love and understanding sustained Rokeya through those losses.

Soon after their marriage Sakhawat was transferred to Bhagalpur from Rangpur. He encouraged Rokeya to mix with women of her class who were staying in Bhagalpur. This opportunity of mixing with educated Hindu and Christian women who enjoyed the privileges of birth or rank like hers showed Rokeya that, given an opportunity, women might lead very different lives from those led by women kept in seclusion. Quite a few of her acquaintances must have been like Shudha Mazumdar—a Hindu contemporary of Rokeya whose life pattern shows many similarities with hers, but with whom Rokeya was apparently not acquainted—whose memoirs show that these women were conscious of their privileged position and possessed a keen sense of their obligations to society, which led them to engage in philanthropic activities.[11] Additionally, Rokeya's extensive reading of books in English that described alternate ways of life sharpened her awareness of the suppression and oppression suffered by Bengali Muslim women. Rokeya was aware that women in all patriarchal societies are exploited and oppressed by men, but her immediate, deep concern was for the group to which she belonged. It was to Sakhawat's great credit that he encouraged his wife to articulate these unconventional thoughts in writing and to publish them. "If my dear husband had not been so supportive, I might never have written or published anything."[12]

Fortunately for her, Sakhawat's thoughts on many social issues were remarkably similar to Rokeya's. Mukunda Deva Mukhopadhyaya, a classmate and close friend of Sakhawat (and son of Bhudeva Mukhopadhyaya, a well-known Hindu educator and writer), reminisced, "As he himself enjoyed the benefits of having an educated wife, he sincerely supported the cause of women's education."[13] However, Rokeya was not destined to enjoy her husband's company for very long. Sakhawat was a diabetic. By 1907 his condition had worsened and his eyesight had begun to fail. Rokeya nursed him and helped him handle his voluminous correspondence, both official and personal, written in English.[14] In 1909 Sakhawat went to Calcutta for medical treatment. He died there on May 3. Before his death he left Rokeya, in addition to her lawful share, a considerable portion of his savings, to be spent on women's education.

That same year Rokeya faithfully carried out her husband's wish by establishing a girls' school in Bhagalpur.[15] However, the husband of Sakhawat's daughter by his first wife (a man orthodox to the point of bigotry) was outraged by the fact that Rokeya not only inherited money but also dared to spend it on women's education. His meanness and hostility became too much even for a person of Rokeya's phenomenal patience and courage. She left Bhagalpur for Calcutta in 1910, but never formally severed connections with the family.[16] In Calcutta she settled down with her mother, who died shortly thereafter. Rokeya's younger sister, Humaira Chowdhury, who was also widowed, became a companion. In 1911 Rokeya opened the Sakhawat Memorial Girls' School in Calcutta with only eight girls in a small building at Number 8, Waliullah Lane. The school, which is still functioning, is a fitting memorial to her wonderful husband as well as to Rokeya herself.

A self-taught woman raised in seclusion, Rokeya had had no experience in a classroom. For the first few days she could not imagine how one teacher could teach several students at the same time. With typical determination, she set about learning the techniques of teaching and of school administration. She visited the Brahmo and Hindu girls' schools in Calcutta and became acquainted with their principals, thus learning from observation how schools are run.[17]

Despite stiff opposition from the traditionalists, Rokeya's tireless hard work and dedication succeeded in slowly attracting students. By the end of 1915, four years after the opening of the school in Calcutta, the number of students had increased from eight to eighty-four, and the school was relocated to a bigger building at 86/A Lower Circular Road. There were only two or three teachers and, to keep the school functioning properly, Rokeya had to work like a machine. She wrote to her cousin, "I find no time at all. By the Grace of Allah, we have 70 students studying in the five classes [the school was a primary school at this time] . . . two horsedrawn carriages. I have to keep an eye on everything. I even have to make sure that the horses are regularly massaged in the evening. And you know what reward I get from my society for all this? My community is busy looking for every little mistake I make."[18]

Rokeya acted as the very soul of moderation on questions of purdah. She hoped that by keeping her school bus well covered she would neutralize the criticism and opposition of the fundamentalists. The narration of the trials and tribulations that Rokeya and the school had to undergo during the trial run of the school bus is illuminating (see Report 47 of *The Secluded*

Ones, reprinted in this volume). The opposition remained active until her death. But she had the courage of her convictions and the faith that moves mountains. Her requests for help and donations were routinely ignored by the rich and influential Muslims of Calcutta, but Rokeya did not give up. By 1930 the school had become a high school, including all ten grades. The curriculum included physical education, handicrafts, sewing, cooking, nursing, home economics, and gardening, in addition to regular courses such as Bangla, English, Urdu, Persian, and Arabic. She laid special emphasis on vocational training for girls which would enable them to become assets rather than liabilities to their families' finances.

The opposition from influential men made Rokeya aware of the need to organize women. She realized that only through organized effort would she be able to build public opinion in favor of women's education, and that solidarity, not isolated effort, was needed. In 1916 she founded the Anjuman-e-Khawatin-e-Islam (Muslim Women's Association). She visited women in their homes to try to interest them in becoming members, but had to tolerate considerable sarcasm and criticism. However, her firm resolve and dedication again triumphed.

The activities she undertook as the guiding spirit of the Anjuman brought her into direct contact with women of poorer classes. Her writing and her school were mainly involved with the upper and middle classes. She has been criticized in recent years for this early bias. But the Anjuman's activities related directly to disadvantaged poor women. It offered financial assistance to poor widows, rescued and sheltered battered wives, helped poor families to marry their daughters, and above all helped poor women to achieve literacy. Rokeya was keenly aware of the elitist nature of formal education in the Bengal of her time. It was clear to her that poor women were impeded by their poverty from acquiring an education. To counter this state of affairs, her association, under her guidance, devised a literacy program for the slum women, both Hindu and Muslim, of Calcutta. To cover the different slum areas in Calcutta, the members formed work teams, visiting the houses of women in the slums to teach them the rudiments of reading, writing, personal hygiene, and child care. Their instruction was given, depending on the linguistic character of the area, in both Bangla and Urdu. Many graduates of the Sakhawat school who volunteered for the project still remember fondly Rokeya's courage, spirit, energy, and inspiring presence.[19]

Until her death in 1932, Rokeya struggled to liberate and educate Bengali Muslim women through her writings, through her school, and through the Anjuman. A review of her literary work and the social context in which she wrote will help us understand what she was struggling to achieve.

Rokeya's literary activities extended over three decades, from 1903 to 1932. Her works, especially her essays, were mainly on a few interrelated topics: 1) women's, especially Bengali Muslim women's, situation; 2) Bengali Muslims and their problems; and 3) Bengali society and its problems. Women were the focal point of Rokeya's thoughts: raising women's consciousness and ensuring women's equal rights and status in society. At the same time she was also deeply concerned about the situation of the Bengali Muslim society of which those women formed an integral part. Similarly she was constantly aware of the greater society—the Bengalis—of which the Bengali Muslims formed a part. Though she was never alienated from her own community, however irritating and unsatisfactory she might have found it, she had a broader vision than some of her Hindu and Muslim contemporaries. Such liberalism is rare in Bengali literature. Indeed, her awareness and concern extended beyond Bengal to include the situation of Indian women more generally and even that of women in other countries. Such a comprehensive worldview is also rare among Bengali authors.

The concern about her own society was a characteristic that she shared with other Muslim authors of the time. The last three decades of the nineteenth century were a time of great stress and change for Indian Muslims. This was partly brought on by the realization that they confronted two powerful rival groups during this period. The Christian English,[20] bearers of an alien culture, held all political power and offered new social and cultural alternatives. The Hindus, quick to respond to the transfer of power from the Muslim Mughals to the British and to learn English, were filling all available government posts, acquiring political and administrative power, and securing the patronage of the colonial rulers. After a prolonged debate between the modernists and the traditionalists which by the 1870s was resolved in favor of the modernists, the Hindus were also in a position to offer new solutions to many social problems common to all Bengalis.[21]

The Muslims, searching for a modus vivendi, also found themselves torn between the traditionalist and modernist approaches. The need for survival as a distinct group and the recognition of their status as a weak minority often drove the Muslims into a defensive stance which sometimes became ultraconservative. But the leadership of Sir Syed Ahmad Khan of Aligarh, described as "the Muslim counterpart of [the Hindu reformer] Ram Mohan Roy, anxious to accept Western Science but without damaging the fabric of Islam,"[22] soon convinced Bengali Muslim leaders such as Nawab Abdul Lateef (1828–1893) and other members of the Mohammadan Literary Society of Calcutta that Bengali Muslim males should acquire modern formal education in order to compete with the Hindus. Their active lobbying compelled the Bengal government to take steps to facilitate the formal education of Muslim males. In 1871, only 14.7 percent of the total Muslim male school-age population attended school; by 1881, the proportion had risen dramatically to 23.8 percent.[23]

The quest for a group identity united Bengali Muslim writers at the turn of the century. This central concern led them to seek their roots in history and tradition, on the one hand, and, on the other, critically to review their present situation. It is interesting to note that until Rokeya raised it, the debaters were virtually silent on one vital social issue: the position of Bengali Muslim women. This silence is the most significant difference between the Bengali Hindu and Muslim quests for identity in the nineteenth century. The most lively and passionate debates between the Hindu traditionalists and modernists raged around issues related to family life and women's position: child marriage, polygamy, widow remarriage, purdah, and women's education.[24] Through the movements launched by the modernists, the Widow Remarriage Act (permitting widows to remarry) was passed in 1856; polygamy began to go out of fashion; the Age of Consent Act, which fixed the minimum legal age of marriage for girls at twelve years, was passed in 1891; in 1866 Brahmo women were allowed to come out of purdah and participate in the weekly congregation; the number of girls' schools rose from 95 in 1863 to 2,238 in 1891, and the number of female students (almost all of them Hindu, Brahmo, and Christian) rose from 2,486 in 1863 to 78,865 in 1891. Indeed, the increasing demand by the younger generation of Hindu and Brahmo men for educated brides compelled even fairly conservative upper- and middle-class Hindu and Brahmo families to send their daughters to school. By 1905 the number of women who had received B.A. and M.A. degrees from Calcutta University totaled thirty. All of them were either Hindu, Brahmo, or Christian; none were Muslim.[25] Why were the Muslims, so eager to catch up with the Hindus and if possible to outstrip them where the education of boys was concerned, so reluctant to emulate them regarding the education of girls? The answer lies perhaps in their attitude toward the need for observance of purdah.

For Muslims, the relaxation of purdah rules—which were enjoined by the Quran and sanctioned by *hadith* (religious traditions based on the sayings of the Prophet)—was a very grave issue. The original instructions, proclaimed in Surah 24 of the Quran, concerned modesty of behavior. A woman was to lower her gaze, to avoid displaying her beauty except to men in permitted categories (husband, father-in-law, brother, sons, stepsons, uncles, children, slaves), to draw a veil or shawl over her head and bosom and avoid attracting attention (for example, by not wearing conspicuous jewelry). Later interpretations and elaborations were directed more toward restricting women's mobility and sexual self-determination.

Fatima Mernissi argues persuasively that the extreme form of seclusion was actually a protective measure, introduced to protect men from women's great powers of seduction which, if unchecked, might succeed in tempting Muslim men to the point of swerving from their allegiance to Allah, their sole Lord and Master. Such breach of loyalty would bring about the much-dreaded *fitna* (chaos) in the *umma* (community of believers)—which is presumably composed of men only, for Islam is a man's religion par excellence. This fear, coupled perhaps with anxiety about paternity, led Muslim men to tighten the restrictions on women's mobility and self-determination.[26] In Rokeya's time, the customs of Muslim purdah permitted few occasions for interaction between men and women. Even in the family, where the two worlds overlapped, strictly followed rules of avoidance precluded transgressions of male and female space.

Moreover, strict observance of purdah rules among the Bengali Muslims, especially among the elite, became important for a socioeconomic reason. Observance of strict purdah not only provided women with separate living quarters at home, but guaranteed their invisibility in public spaces through covered transport and the *burqa*. These measures involved considerable expense which only the affluent could afford. Purdah observance quickly became a status symbol. Thus the same motive, status, that had encouraged upper-class Muslim families in Rokeya's time to send their sons to progressive schools stood in the way of their daughters' modernization.

The resultant cultural and intellectual gap, forever widening, between the men and women of the Muslim upper middle class did not seem to concern Muslim men. Nor did the improvement in the status and situation of Hindu and Brahmo women resulting from their access to education seem to perturb Muslim men greatly. But Rokeya realized the adverse effects of the cultural deprivation on the already inferior status of Muslim women. She led a campaign to persuade her society to change its attitude toward women.

The five articles that Rokeya published in 1903–4—"Strijatir Abanati" ("The Degradation of Women"), "Ardhangi" ("The Female Half"), "Sugrihini" ("The Good Housewife"), "Borka" ("The Cloak"), and "Griha" ("Home")—might be considered her preliminary statement of the problem of purdah. The bulk of her later work elaborated and substantiated the thesis presented in these articles, which were collected and published in the book *Motichur* (1908). The essays illustrate her beliefs and her strategy as an advocate of the women's cause. Rokeya argued as follows:

1. Though at present economically dependent on men for historical reasons, women are not innately inferior to them mentally or spiritually. Given equal opportunity, they can easily prove themselves men's equal in mental and spiritual endowments.

2. By confining women to the household, men deliberately deprive women of equal opportunity to cultivate their minds and to engage in gainful employment, thus making them dependent and inferior in status.
3. Men perpetuate their domination of women through several mechanisms of social control, chief among which are seclusion and socialization.
4. They further deprive women from exercising their lawful rights by manipulating laws that are man-made and by taking advantage of women's ignorance and vulnerability.
5. The unjust and immoral practice of deliberately depriving half the society of the opportunity of healthy and natural growth is detrimental to the society as a whole.
6. This deprivation and close confinement also make women deficient in reasoning, ignorant, and physically weak, thus rendering them unfit for properly executing their socially ascribed roles as housewives and mothers.
7. The only effective and morally right solution to this deplorable state of affairs is to give women access to education, emancipation from purdah being a precondition.
8. Finally, the benefits accrued by society (including men) would be immense, for educated women would be responsible in and useful to the society.

Certain characteristics distinguish Rokeya as an advocate for women. First, she was a Muslim and a woman. The other initiators of debate about women, such as Raja Ram Mohan Roy, a Brahmo, and Ishwar Chandra Vidyasagar, a Hindu, were male. Rokeya's tone was more passionate and angry than theirs.[27] Second, men like Roy and Vidyasagar were quickly and ably supported by other social reformers and notable figures like the Tagores.[28] Indeed, women of the Tagore family soon joined the debate and set an example for other women.[29] Rokeya had to struggle a long time before gaining support from influential people of her society. The last and most important difference between Rokeya and other advocates for women is that, of all these reformers, Rokeya alone challenged the accepted notions of male superiority.

Rokeya was aware that in order to establish her case, she would have to refute the counterarguments of the traditionalists and to make women themselves aware of the need for change. Angry though she often was, Rokeya rarely let herself get carried away by her emotions. Her rational bent of mind and uncommon measure of common sense showed her that women themselves must bear some responsibility for consenting to be victimized and oppressed in silence.

Rokeya knew that the fundamentalists rested their case for innate male superiority on the belief in divine ordination, the evidence for which was to be found in religious texts; for example, in the story of creation in the Semitic (Judeo-Christian-Islamic) religious texts and in the strictures of Manu for male guardianship of women in Hindu texts. The strictures of Manu state that a woman is not fit to take care of herself; in childhood her father, in youth her husband, and in old age her son are her legal guardians.

On the improbability of divine ordination Rokeya wrote, referring to the Islamic legal stand of recognizing two women as equivalent to one man: "Had God Himself intended women to be inferior, He would have ordained it so that mothers would have given birth to daughters at the end of the fifth month of pregnancy. The supply of mother's milk would naturally have been half of that in case of a son. But that is not the case. How can it be? Is not God just and most merciful?"[30] She concluded that "men are using religion as an excuse to dominate us at present. . . . Therefore we should not submit quietly to such oppression in the name of religion."[31] This required great courage on Rokeya's part, for she was questioning a legal position based on the text of the Quran itself. While Muslim scholars and jurists do not hesitate to debate the *hadith*—the body of traditions based on sayings or actions of the Prophet and his companions—few Muslims dare to challenge the revealed text of the Quran which they are expected to accept unconditionally.

The traditionalist reluctance to educate women was voiced thus: Men have to go to school, learn English, and get a degree because they have to get jobs in order to support their families; a woman who is going to stay home, look after the household, and be economically dependent on a man would find education irrelevant. Rokeya had very different ideas of what the nature and purpose of education were. According to her, education was "the development of the God-given faculties by regular exercise of these faculties. Merely passing an examination and getting a degree does not constitute real education, in our opinion."[32] The point of education is not to get a job. The ultimate purpose of education for human beings, regardless of sex, is self-realization, the fullest development of their potential as human beings. That is why women have as much right as men to education.

What would this education do for women? According to Rokeya, a proper education would teach them "to acquire knowledge in the different branches of science and arts. . . . They would learn to love their country. . . . It would include physical education so that they are not frail. Special emphasis would be laid on that training which would enable them to be financially independent of men."[33] She repeatedly emphasized the need to teach women chemistry, botany, horticulture, personal hygiene, health care, nutrition, physical education, gymnastics, and painting and other fine arts. Of all the Bengali reformers, she seems to have been the only one who clearly understood that economic independence is the first prerequisite of women's liberation. She wrote: "Some say that women tolerate oppression from men because they depend on men's earning. They are right."[34] She proposed that women start working: "If our liberation from male domination depends on our ability to earn independently, then we should begin. We should be lawyers, magistrates, judges, clerks. . . . The sort of labour we put in our households can bring us wages if we use it outside."[35] And she extended her attention beyond the range of these obviously middle-class jobs, writing that "in addition to these jobs, we should consider the opportunities offered by agriculture."[36]

Rokeya knew that to be liberated, a woman must come out of seclusion, but she also knew that coming out of seclusion did not mean that liberation would necessarily follow. She saw that a woman might move about unveiled without being liberated, and that a woman would be truly liberated only when she was capable of thinking and making decisions independently. Rokeya gave an example:

Recently we see the Parsi* women moving about unveiled, but are they truly free from mental slavery? Certainly not! Their unveiling is not a result of their own decision. The Parsi men have dragged their women out of purdah in a blind imitation of the Europeans. It does not show any initiative of their women. They are as lifeless as they were before. When their men kept them in seclusion they stayed there. When the men dragged them out by their "nose-rings" they came out. That cannot be called an achievement by women.[37]

To Rokeya this mental slavery was the most harmful aspect of prolonged domination by men. Women's faculty of reasoning would inevitably atrophy in a system that denied them the opportunity to exercise it. Such a mental state permits the perpetuation of slavery. Rokeya compared this state to an addiction: "How strong habits are! We desire the badges of slavery [jewelry] since we are accustomed to slavery just as an alcoholic hankers after a drink! . . . Your jewelry, of which you are so proud, is nothing but badges of slavery. Prisoners wear handcuffs made of iron, we wear bracelets made of gold or silver. Our gem-studded chokers are probably imitated from dog-collars."[38]

The relationship between a woman socialized to be dependent on men and on her husband in particular, Rokeya contended, is bound to be that of master and slave, no matter what flattering terms men used to denote it. She reminded her readers that the Bengali term for husband, *swami*, literally means "master." She elaborated her point by referring to Rama and Sita, the couple extolled as ideal in the Hindu epic *Ramayana*:

Rama's relationship with Sita . . . is exactly that of a boy and his favorite doll. A boy may be terribly fond of his toy; he may miss it awfully when he is away from it . . . ; if it is stolen, he may be mad at the stealer; he may be overjoyed when he gets it back yet

---

*The small Parsi community in South Asia is descended from Persian Zoroastrians, who migrated to India many centuries ago. They retain their distinctive religion, live mainly in western India, and tend to marry within the group. Parsis were among the first to work with the British during colonial times, to accept English education, and to allow women to wear western dress.

he may throw it in the mud the next moment for no good reason at all—but the doll does not do anything for it is lifeless. . . . In the Ramayana, Rama acts in a similar fashion and demonstrates fully his status as Sita's *swami*, but what about Sita? Did Rama ever act in a way which showed that Sita also has feelings?[39]

Rokeya was convinced that only a truly educated and liberated woman deserves to be an equal partner of her husband. She compared a household where such a relationship exists with a well-sprung carriage, its wheels (husband and wife) running smoothly, at a well-coordinated pace, neither one advancing ahead of the other. Certainly this is an infinitely better image than that presented by the majority of couples of the time, who exhibited an enormous cultural and educational gap and lack of communication. She transposed the intellectual image to a physical one and made fun of it:

> Dear reader, take a look at yourself in the mirror. Your right side is the male half and the left side is female. . . . Your right arm is thirty inches long and quite strong. Your left arm is twenty-four inches long and thin. . . . The right shoulder reaches to five feet while the left shoulder reaches up to only four feet. . . . How do you like the image you present?[40]

Rokeya reserved the argument most likely to convince opponents of women's education for the last salvo, showing how necessary formal education is for the smooth and efficient running of a modern household. To keep pace with the demands of changing times, a good housewife needed to know so much more than what was taught her—a few pages of Urdu primer, very simple arithmetic, and five hundred recipes for preserves and pickles, but nothing about nutrition, diet, nursing, or child psychology, not to mention other subjects. "Education is the first requisite for motherhood, because a mother is the first and the most important teacher and trainer of a child."[41] This was a familiar argument, used by the non-Muslim Bengali reformers before Rokeya. It was an argument that even the traditionalists found hard to refute. Luckily for Rokeya's conscience, she sincerely believed in the significance of the early environment in molding human character and in the central role a mother plays in that setting. Consequently she was able to put her conviction behind the argument.

Rokeya anticipated the likelihood of the proponents of orthodoxy considering her a radical; she certainly wrote like one. However, she opposed extreme measures. In fact, she was against the excesses of seclusion, which obstructed women's education and development as human beings, but was not against the principles of purdah, which were concerned with modesty and decorum. She argued: "Veiling is not natural, it is ethical. Animals have no veils."[42] Rokeya pointed out that veiling, in the sense of protecting oneself from public exposure, was present in all civilized societies. "By purdah I mean covering the body well, not staying confined."[43] On the question of what sort of purdah might be desirable, she had a ready answer: "We shall keep necessary and moderate purdah. . . . This sort of purdah would not be an obstacle to feminine education. With separate girls' schools and adequate teachers we could both maintain the obligatory minimum of purdah and still educate our women."[44]

All her life she herself used the burqa when appearing in public. In her schools and among friends and relatives, she covered her head by the *anchal* (end) of her sari (see frontispiece), following the fashion of other educated women of her time. Rather anticlimactic? Slightly contradictory? Well, no. It was an eminently practical stand, taken by a woman who, despite a strong commitment to ideals and causes, had a strong streak of pragmatism and a clear understanding of the realities of life. Perhaps that is why she succeeded as an activist.

Though her main concern was the situation and status of Muslim women, she was too well informed to remain unaware of the exploitation and oppression of women in other societies. In *The Secluded Ones*, her reports include descriptions of the Hindu custom of purdah also. And she realized, unlike many of her Indian sisters, that Western women, despite their apparent freedom, were the victims of Western men who were aided by man-made laws. In her "Delicia Hatya" ("Murder of Delicia," a free translation of a story written by the popular Victorian novelist Marie Corelli), she highlighted this aspect of Western life: "Alas, law aids those who have money and influence. It is not meant to help vulnerable women like us."[45] A few incidents in *Padmaraga*, her novel, based on real life stories related by the Hindu and Christian teachers of the Sakhawat Memorial School, show how the women of these communities were oppressed by their guardians.

As mentioned earlier, Rokeya did not believe that the situation of women could be changed in isolation from the situation of the whole society. Her society ultimately included the whole Indian society. It is surprising to find that this self-taught woman raised in seclusion rose above narrow sectarian feelings and stated, with firm conviction, "Remember, we are Indians first, Hindu, Muslim, Sikh afterwards. It is the duty of every good housewife to make her family members aware of this."[46] Surprising because after the establishment of the Muslim League in 1906, to protect and promote the legal and political rights of Muslims, Muslim political allegiance gradually moved from secular interests to sectarian ones. During her lifetime there were terrible Hindu–Muslim riots, and in 1930 Iqbal, the well-known Muslim poet who wrote in Urdu, proposed the establishment of a separate Muslim state. Rokeya does not seem to have been committed to this separatism. But this is certainly not any indication of a lack of interest in political issues, as she had very strong political opinions. In fact, such a conscious and "aware" citizen could hardly have avoided feeling oppressed under colonial rule. In a letter congratulating the editor of the English daily the *Mussalman* on the eve of its twentieth anniversary, she wrote (in English): "Anybody who has some experience of public work knows very well how difficult it is to serve one's country, specially when the interests of the people clash with those of their Governments."[47] Rokeya's own clash with vested interests in her male-dominated society became more vehement when her dual career of publicist and activist in the women's cause gathered steam after her husband's death.

Eighty years have passed since the publication of "Sultana's Dream," well over fifty years since Rokeya's death. During her lifetime, her work as both a publicist and an activist evoked intense hostility and great admiration. Some of her contemporaries called her a shameless woman, a misanthrope, a radical misguided by the proselytizing propaganda of Christian missionaries, and a sexist. Her works were called inflammatory pamphlets designed to stir up insubordination among women. Others called her the soul and spirit of modern Muslim Bengal personified, the pride of her society, the harbinger of dawn. Within a short time after her death, younger male, and some female, contemporaries of Rokeya became powerful advocates for her cause. The modernization of Turkey and the emancipation of Turkish women from seclusion following the deposition of the Sultan in 1911 greatly influenced the Bengali Muslims. Ismail Hussain Siraji (1880–1931), an influential journalist who went to Turkey in 1912 and was impressed by the contribution of Turkish women to the nation-building efforts; male authors like the well-known poet Nazrul Islam, Moniruzzaman Islamabadi, and Ibrahim Khan; and women like Shamsunnahar Mahmud, the educator, and Begum Sufia Kamal, the poet, were all articulate advocates for women's education and the moderation of purdah. Their combined efforts gradually changed the attitude of upper-class Muslims toward purdah. Women from the upper and middle classes slowly came out of seclusion to acquire formal education and join various professions.

How do modern Bangladeshis view Rokeya? They usually pay lip service to her memory on the anniversary of her death. True, some of her essays continue to be included in the school syllabus for the Bangla language course. It is interesting to note, however, that the essays selected are always those written on general social problems, not the women-specific ones discussed here. Her writings became rare until the Bangla Academy took the trouble of publishing *Rokeya Racanavali* in 1973, soon after Bangladesh came into being. Indeed, until the declaration of the United Nations Decade for Women (1975–1985), interest in studying her works was very limited. Since 1981, however, Rokeya has received attention from scholars (both male and female) studying the situation of Bangladeshi women. The current generation of feminists has found that despite her limitations (chiefly her middle-class bias), the substance of Rokeya's arguments is still very pertinent, especially in view of the recent resurgence of fundamentalism in many Muslim countries. Her dream of empowering women is a dream they also share and work for. In recent seminars marking the end of the United

Nations Decade for Women, angry statements were made about the negligence shown by her society in not erecting a suitable public monument in recognition of Rokeya's contributions. But why is a monument necessary when every educated Bangladeshi woman is a living memorial to this extraordinary woman?

Notes to Rokeya: An Introduction to Her Life

1. Rokeya Sakhawat Hossain, *Rokeya Racanavali* (Dhaka: Bangla Academy, 1973), p. 319. All translations of quotations from this volume are by Roushan Jahan from the original Bangla text.

2. Motahar Hossain Sufi, *Begum Rokeya: Jivan O Sahitya* (*Begum Rokeya: Life and Works*) (Dhaka: University Press Ltd., 1986), p. 3.

3. The dedication is not included in the *Rokeya Racanavali* and consequently did not form a part of Roushan Jahan's *Inside Seclusion: The Avarodhbasini of Rokeya Sakhawat Hossain*, which was published by Women for Women, Dhaka, in 1981. The edition of *Avarodhbasini* printed by the Nari Kalyan Sangstha of Dhaka in 1982 does carry this dedication to her mother.

4. Laila Zaman, *Rokeya Sakhawat Hossain* (Dhaka: Bangla Academy, 1987), p. 10, quoted from Dr. Muhammad Shamsul Alam, *Begum Rokeya Sakhawat Hossain: Jivani O Sahitya Karma* (*Begum Rokeya Sakhawat Hossain: Life and Literary Works*), Ph.D. diss., Chittagong University, 1985.

5. Rokeya Sakhawat Hossain, "Lukano Ratan" ("Hidden Treasure"), in *Rokeya Racanavali*, pp. 285–86.

6. Ibid., p. 76.

7. Shamsunnahar Mahmud, *Rokeya Jivani* (*Biography of Rokeya*) (Dacca: School Text Book Board, 1958), p. 18.

8. Rokeya Sakhawat Hossain, *Rokeya Racanavali*, p. 319.

9. Motahar Hossain Sufi, *Begum Rokeya*, p. 10.

10. There is some confusion about the exact age of Rokeya at the time of her wedding. In the introduction to her collected letters, the editor calculated that Rokeya was eighteen at the time (*Patre Rokeya Pariciti* [*Knowing Rokeya through Her Letters*], ed. Moshfequa Mahmud [Dacca: Bangla Academy, 1965], p. 2). However, in the dedication to *Motichur, Part Two*, Rokeya herself states that she stayed in Bhagalpur, where she moved soon after the wedding, for fourteen years. As she left Bhagalpur for Calcutta in 1910, we are persuaded to conclude that Rokeya was married in 1896, when she was sixteen.

11. Shudha Mazumdar, *A Pattern of Life: The Memoirs of an Indian Woman*, ed. Geraldine H. Forbes (Columbia, Mo.: South Asia Books and New Delhi: Manohar Book Service, 1977).

12. Rokeya Sakhawat Hossain, *Rokeya Rancanavali.*

13. Ibid., p. 8, quoted from Mukunda Deva Mukhopadhyaya, *Amar Dekha Lok (People I Have Seen).*

14. Ibid., p. 8.

15. There is a widespread notion that Rokeya's school was the first to be established by a Muslim woman to educate Muslim girls. The first school for Muslim girls was established in 1897 in Calcutta under the patronage of Begum Ferdous Mahal, the Begum of the Nawab of Murshidabad. In 1909, another school for Muslim girls was founded under the patronage of Khojesta Akhtar Banu of the Suhrawardy family. Nothing much is known about the role of these schools in spreading education among Muslim girls of Calcutta. Credit for being the first Muslim woman to establish a girls' school (not specifically limited to Muslim girls, however) in Bengal belongs to Nawab Faizunnessa, the famous zemindar, social worker, and writer of Comilla. This school was established in 1873, seven years before Rokeya's birth (Morshed Shafiul Hasan, *Begum Rokeya: Samaya O Sahitya [Begum Rokeya: Time and Literary Works]* [Dhaka: Bangla Academy, 1982], pp. 14, 36). As a former student of this excellent school, I am happy to note that the Faizunnessa Girls' High School is still functioning as one of the top girls' schools in Bangladesh.

16. In *The Secluded Ones*, Report Eleven describes the pre-wedding confinement of the daughters of this stepdaughter. Rokeya attended the wedding ceremony in 1926. Report Twenty-five describes incidents from an earlier visit.

17. Shamsunnahar Mahmud, "Begum Rokeya Sakhawat Hossain," *The Begum*, February 16, 1964, p. 29. For a discussion of the lives of Brahmo women, see Meredith Borthwick, *The Changing Role of Women in Bengal, 1849–1905* (Princeton, N.J.: Princeton University Press, 1984).

18. Motahar Hossain Sufi, *Begum Rokeya*, p. 36.

19. Roushan Jahan, *Inside Seclusion*, p. 19.

20. In South Asian usage, the term *English* applies to all members of the English-speaking colonial ruling class.

21. For more on the debate in literary circles, see Ghulam Murshid's *The Reluctant Debutante: Response of Bengali Women to Modernization* (Rajshahi: Rajshahi University, 1983).

22. Michael Edwardes, *Raj: The Story of British India* (London: Pan Books, 1969), p. 302. Raja Ram Mohan Roy (1774–1833) was a Hindu social and religious reformer who founded the Brahmo Samaj in 1828 as a religious association; it later became a reform movement. It was influenced by Unitarianism and many of its members tried consciously to emulate the fashions and manners of the English colonial rulers.

23. Anisuzzaman, *Muslim Manos O Bangla Sahitya* (*Muslim Thought and Bengali Literature*) (Dacca: Dacca University, 1964), p. 90.

24. In the era under discussion, polygamy was widely prevalent, especially among high-caste Brahmins. Child marriage was widely practiced; most girls were married off before they were nine years old. As marriage was regarded as a sacrament, widows were not permitted to remarry. Men, however, could marry as often as they liked. Divorce was not allowed. Purdah was strictly observed even by the Hindus and obtructed women's formal schooling.

25. Ghulam Murshid, *The Reluctant Debutante*, pp. 43, 253–54.

26. Fatima Mernissi, *Beyond the Veil: Male–Female Dynamics in a Modern Muslim Society* (Cambridge, Mass.: Schenkman Publishing, 1975).

27. See Patricia Meyer Spacks, *The Female Imagination* (New York: Knopf, 1975), for a detailed discussion of anger in English and U.S. women authors.

28. The Tagores were a rich and influential Brahmo family of Calcutta. Many of them were talented poets, novelists, singers, and fashion trendsetters. The best known of them all was Rabindranath Tagore, poet, educator, painter, and the first Indian to win the Nobel prize for literature (in 1913).

29. Ghulam Murshid, *The Reluctant Debutante*. See also Chitra Deb, *Thakurbarir Andarmahale* (*In the Inner Apartments of the Tagore House*) (Calcutta: Ananda Publishers, 1980).

30. Rokeya Sakhawat Hossain, *Rokeya Racanavali*, p. 43.

31. Introduction to ibid., p. 13.

32. "Strijatir Abanati" ("The Degradation of Women"), in ibid., p. 27.

33. "Padmaraga" ("Ruby"), in ibid., p. 329.

34. "Strijatir Abanati," in ibid., p. 28.

35. Ibid., pp. 29–30.

36. Ibid., p. 30.

37. Ibid., p. 36.

38. Ibid., p. 20.

39. "Ardhongi" ("The Female Half"), in ibid., p. 37.

40. Ibid., p. 38.

41. "Sugrihini" ("The Good Housewife"), in ibid., p. 53.

42. "Borka" ("The Veil"), in ibid., p. 57.

43. Ibid., p. 57.

44. Ibid, pp. 60–62.

45. "Delicia Hatya," in ibid., p. 170.

46. "Sugrihini," in ibid., p. 54.

47. Quoted in Motahar Hossain Sufi, *Begum Rokeya*, p. 1.

Afterword
Caging the Lion:
A Fable for Our Time

Hanna Papanek

Rokeya Sakhawat Hossain's story, written so long ago, is just right for our time, a time when social and religious movements in many countries and many religions want to use women, once again, to show that men are right-minded. Fundamentalist Christians, Muslims, Hindus, Jews, and Buddhists of many kinds are propagating similar messages in many parts of the world. It all seems so simple: There is something wrong in the world and one way to fix it is to put women "in their place," a place most women would not choose for themselves.

Rokeya's most important message speaks directly to this point. She rebukes women for failing to recognize and act on their self-interest in a passage where the Guide tells the Dreamer:

> "Why do you allow yourselves to be shut up? You have neglected the duty you owe to yourselves and you have lost your natural rights by shutting your eyes to your own interests."

This must have been heady advice to Rokeya's readers and explains her passionate commitment to female education. It is no less relevant today.

The quiet revolution in women's lives—the emancipation and education of more than a few—which was once safely launched is again endangered today by indirect threats to women's ability to perceive and choose their options. To be sure, more women are going to school in countries around the world and more women are taking jobs outside the home. But at the same time, and in the same places where educational enrollments and employment figures are rising, there are social and religious movements that seek to limit women's options in other ways. In the United States, for example, movements that seek to prohibit all women's access to abortion and contraception, and similar movements in parts of Europe that oppose the granting of divorces, all use religious traditions as a basis for trying to change public morality and private behavior.

Rokeya's specific concern was the practice of purdah among the Muslims of Bengal; in this essay, I take a somewhat broader view. It is not easy to define *purdah*; the word is a kind of shorthand for practices that might include, depending on choices made by families, veiling the face, wearing a concealing cloak, living in secluded quarters, and never meeting men outside the family. It is making a comeback: Veiling is being revived in a number of countries, and some women are carefully limiting their contacts with men. Even where veiling has not been widely revived, other changes in women's dress (long skirts, long sleeves, head coverings) signal change in belief and practice.

Seen from a global and historical perspective, the rejection of purdah and its recent partial revival present a striking paradox. Both rejection and revival are founded on ideas of national identity and stress the central importance of women in the symbolism of nationhood. Both show how events that seem unrelated to personal life—large changes in economic, political, and social structures at the level of the nation-state—are reflected in dramatic changes in self-perception and the public presentation of the self.

In the first half of this century, the emancipation of women and the rejection of veiling were closely related to national movements for independence from colonial rule. Leaders of nationalist movements often encouraged women to join and to appear more freely in public, even if they had not been in seclusion and only custom or modesty had prevented their participation. Among Indian Muslims, for example, women's participation in the nationalist movement, not only as followers but also as leaders, was paralleled by their gradual emergence from purdah. The modernized, educated elite in the former colonies, which included Muslims, Hindus, and Christians, were also interested in convincing rulers that they were ready to govern their own countries. Releasing women from seclusion, if that had been the practice, was part of the process of demonstrating their modernity and often reflected a desire to emulate the colonial rulers in order to become equally strong.[1]

In the second half of the twentieth century, well after most nations had achieved independence from colonial rule (in the 1940s and 1950s), a revival of veiling and the introduction or reintroduction of "modest" dress are taking place in many Asian and African countries, particularly those with large Muslim populations. Among Muslims, these changes are occurring in the context of a great religious tradition. They are part of a new nationalism, a reaffirmation of national identity in the idiom of a revitalized Islam, a rejection of values perceived as "Western" and alien to the nation's needs. Changes in the public demeanor of women are important signals of conformity to these new ideas; equally important, they are convenient ways of communicating them to a wider audience. But these changes are more than superficial: Many women show a renewed interest in religious activities and are sometimes breaking new ground by participating in activities, such as religious studies, in which few women have been openly active in the past.

Movements that encourage the revival of purdah in Muslim populations also have a direct counterpart in other parts of the world. They involve other great religious traditions, including Christianity, Hinduism, and Judaism. In the United States and parts of Europe, for example, movements that seek to prohibit access to abortion, contraception, and divorce use religious traditions as a basis for trying to achieve changes in public morality and private behavior. These movements usually seek to impose their own ideology of womanhood on a broader public, just as do many movements that encourage the revival of purdah. These parallels cannot be overlooked for they are global in scope and meaning.

The sexual and reproductive powers of women are central to the efforts of these new movements, regardless of their religious or ideological context. The connection is obvious in the case of movements to limit contraception and abortion; it is more indirect in the case of purdah, but fears of sexual freedom and moral chaos are generally part of the appeal made by proponents of purdah. Issues involving sexuality and reproduction are excellent mobilizing devices to appeal to large constituencies, because most people have opinions on them even if they do not participate actively in other kinds of political or social movements. The revival of veiling, therefore, is not an isolated phenomenon in a distant part of the world—it has its direct counterparts in countries where most people have never heard of purdah.

Both kinds of movements also share another characteristic: the appeal to religious prescriptions said to be ancient and unchanging. In fact, these prescriptions are less solidly grounded than they appear and are usually the subject of intense controversy. Purdah, for example, is by no means universal in Muslim populations, and, where it does exist, it varies widely in form and severity. It has changed greatly over time in different countries and has never been a stable institution. Similarly, in other religions, ideas about abortion and contraception have varied over time, even in the last few centuries, but are presented as if they have always existed in precisely their present form.

These similarities suggest the obvious: Social and religious movements construct what might be called *synthetic traditions* to embody the goals and needs of the present, clothed in ancient garb to make them more powerful. They are obviously open to challenge but, especially in the case of synthetic traditions that directly affect women, challenges have often been slow in coming.

One particular issue that complicates the development of challenges to new synthetic traditions involving women presents serious difficulties. Running like a common thread through the ideas of movements to revive veiling and limit reproductive rights is the idea of women's "special" status. This idea shows women as very different from men, as "closer to nature," better equipped than men to be "carriers of tradition," and therefore indispensable to family life in a "special" role. Religious rituals often reinforce the specialization. Almost inevitably, the concept of women's "special" status is linked to ideas of male–female "complementarity" rather than to equality.

Ideas about women's special nature are shared by many

women, in part because they can also be sources of great strength. The new synthetic traditions, such as those associated with the revival of purdah, emphasize this source of strength and usually link it to women's renewed religious commitment. But others in these same countries continue to feel that anything that sets women apart will limit women's participation in public and private life. Ideas about male–female complementarity may be only another way of stressing women's dependence on men in social, economic, and legal realms.

Lack of clarity about women's special status may make it harder to understand what is happening with respect to the new synthetic traditions in many countries. In view of the ambivalences and ambiguities aroused by conflicting views on these issues, it is also becoming more difficult to analyze why women and families play such central roles in social and religious change or how such issues are used in mobilization efforts by new political and social movements.

Rokeya's story itself and the closer look at purdah that it brings with it can be among the starting points in trying to understand these new changes.

She Who Sits Behind the Curtain

Rokeya wrote as a Muslim about purdah among Muslims in Bengal (present-day Bangladesh and the Indian state of West Bengal), but it is hard to reconstruct life in purdah only from her utopian mirror images. What does it really mean to "be in purdah" or, even if not veiled, to live in a society where some women are in purdah? Some of the evidence can be read in *The Secluded Ones*—but things have changed and Rokeya, after all, wrote as an activist against a custom she hated.

In thinking about purdah, both its rejection and its revival, we must pay attention to the vast differences among the women who observe it. Purdah is not monolithic, although this is the way it is usually seen in countries where it is unknown, and moralists and observers have usually presented it in very simplistic form, as a single set of customs.

In the sections that follow, I present purdah from many angles, seen through a sort of kaleidoscope, before going on to a discussion of the larger context within which purdah functions in South Asia (India, Pakistan, Bangladesh, Nepal, and Sri Lanka). Even if there were no veiling at all, I believe, the prevailing "family ideology" would continue to constrain both women and men. "Abolishing" the family is patently absurd in societies based on functioning families, but we certainly need new ways of asking new questions about the nature of family structures and ideologies. The study of purdah provides an opportunity to do so.

A woman in purdah is often called *pardanashin*—"she who sits behind the curtain." The word *parda* (*purdah* is the common Anglicized form) means "curtain," but the dictionary definition goes far beyond this meaning. To cite only a few selected meanings from a great dictionary of Urdu and Hindi:

> *parda* . . . A curtain, screen, cover, veil . . . secrecy, privacy, modesty; seclusion, concealment; secret, mystery, reticence, reserve; screen, shelter, pretext . . .
> *parda chorna* . . . to drop the curtain or veil; to lay aside concealment; to come into public . . .[2]

The *zenana*, or women's part of the house, was the area where the women of purdah-observing families spent their lives, except when they went on visits to other women in their own zenanas. The term is less widely used today but this internal arrangement of houses may still exist, perhaps in modified form, where purdah observance is strict. The real significance of the zenana and *mardana* (men's quarters) lies in the spatial separation between the women of the house and those males with whom they cannot have contact (see below). The forms of purdah observance include spatial separation, the wearing of special garments, several kinds of *portable seclusion* in which women can move about in public, and certain kinds of body language. Much has been written about the form and substance of purdah in South Asia; here I will summarize only enough to make Rokeya's story understandable to readers unfamiliar with purdah and its implications.[3]

Spatial separation among South Asian Muslims involves setting aside a part of the home for the exclusive use of women and those men before whom they do not observe purdah. Male guests outside the permitted categories of close relatives (whom

Rokeya calls "sacred relations") must stay outside this part of the home. Usually this means that male guests of the men of the family sit in a separate room near the front of the house, on a veranda, or on seats in the open courtyard. In the larger homes of better-off families, especially earlier in this century, typical Muslim houses contained a separate inner courtyard around which rooms opened onto a veranda. These were rooms for sleeping, as in the warm climate of South Asia many other activities took place in the open air, in the courtyard, or on the open veranda. Women and children spent their days in this part of the house which usually also contained the kitchen; men of the family entered it for meals and at night; female servants (and perhaps young boys working for the family) also went in and out but adult male servants did not. This was the type of house in which my friend Hamida Khala, whose struggle with purdah I will describe in the next section, grew up in the years around World War I.

Women living in strict purdah could travel outside their homes in a *doli* (palanquin), a kind of cloth tent attached to four wooden poles carried by strong men. It is still used in rural areas of South Asia, especially on ceremonial occasions such as weddings, but automobiles are now used by those who can afford them. Cars may have tinted or curtained windows. Some extremely strict families still insist that the path from car to house be shielded from public view by people holding up long sheets on both sides of the path, even though the women are heavily veiled, but this is an uncommon practice.

In addition to the segregation achieved by spatial separation within the home and in segregated transport, there are also covering garments that provide what I think of as portable seclusion. This is especially important for those families who crave the respectability conferred by purdah but cannot afford to keep women off the streets altogether and do not have segregated transport. In South Asia, Muslim women in purdah wear the *burqa*, a clumsy garment meant to conceal the female face and body. Wearing the burqa is what is usually described as "being veiled," but this term is really a misnomer: Many people unfamiliar with purdah think of a veil as a transparent piece of gauze over the face that adds to a woman's allure. The burqa is more like a tent, worn over a woman's clothes like an overcoat. It covers the person from the top of the head to the wrists and the ankles. There are various designs for burqas, as fashions change quickly; thirty years ago, in the cities of Pakistan, the more traditional white cotton model was worn by poorer women while middle-class pardanashin wore dark blue or black models made of synthetic fabrics. Nowadays, these garments come in many colors and in different designs. Most have a double layer of material in front of the face, not quite transparent, which the wearer can lift up if she wishes. Women who wear the burqa but who do not cover their faces are considered to observe "open-face purdah"; at one time this was quite common in Pakistani cities and is related to the controversy over whether the Quran requires women to veil their faces.

The use of the burqa is not universal among pardanashin, even in South Asia, and forms of covering women's bodies and faces are often quite different in other countries. Nowadays, sunglasses are often worn to provide a kind of partial anonymity, sometimes together with covering garments, sometimes not. The form of purdah observance is also different in rural areas than in cities, although the urban burqa has spread widely through the countryside. Village women in many parts of South Asia still do not use it but shield their faces, if they observe purdah, with shawls. The burqa itself seems to have been unknown in India until some time in the nineteenth century.

The rules for purdah observance among Muslims are derived from the Quran, which Muslims believe to be the word of God. Verses in the Quran specify the men with whom women may interact, including husbands, fathers, fathers-in-law, brothers, nephews, and sons.[4] Basically, these are the members of the extended kin group and these rules essentially set up boundaries between the family and the rest of the society. The implementation of the rules of purdah, elaborated in the commentaries on the Quran (*hadith*), has been the subject of debate among Muslims for centuries and this debate continues today. Among the points at issue are the forms of observance—for example, whether or not women should be required to cover their faces—rather than the boundaries of the group within which contact is not limited by purdah.

A complicating feature of South Asian society is that some Hindu castes, especially in north and central India, also observe customs that involve veiling and spatial separation. These customs are sometimes called purdah and sometimes referred to otherwise.[5] Hindu practices follow very different rules, in terms of both form and substance, but there is some overlap between Hindu and Muslim practices. In the most general sense, Hindu purdah emphasizes respect relations within the family into which women marry and the boundaries between women's natal and marital families. Hindu women, in purdah-observing communities, must veil their faces before their husbands' elder male relatives and, by extension, before all elder males in the village into which brides come as strangers. They do not veil in their natal villages before marriage nor when they return on visits home as married women. Muslim practices, by contrast, set the family somewhat apart from the wider society by limiting the interactions of all women with all men who are not part of the family. In both cases purdah observance marks social boundaries, but these boundaries mark out different grounds.

Both Muslim and Hindu purdah are potent instruments for teaching women their place in the social order. In both cases, purdah rules communicate how women must behave and with whom they may interact. But Muslim and Hindu purdah are very different in both ideology and practice. The differences between them reflect differences in social organization between these groups in South Asian society. Muslim women often learn to be afraid of the world beyond the home and venture out only reluctantly, especially where purdah is strictly observed.[6] About Hindu veiling practices in a north Indian village, the anthropologist Ursula Sharma notes that purdah teaches a woman "the distinction between those situations in which she ought to be passive and submissive and those in which some degree of responsible activity and control are allowed her."[7]

Parentally arranged marriages are still the norm throughout South Asia, and the norms governing the arrangement of marriages are highly relevant to the norms of purdah among Muslims and Hindus. Muslims tend to prefer marriages within a known circle of families, and in some instances there are strong preferences to arrange marriages among cousins, especially between women and cousins on their father's side. Outside South Asia (among the Bedouins of northern Egypt, for example) this preference for paternal cousin marriage is so strong that any other choice faces staunch opposition.[8] Among north Indian Hindus, by contrast, it is customary to marry women into families of the same caste, preferably the same subcaste but not closely related, and living in somewhat distant villages in the same region. Hindu women, therefore, come into the marital home as strangers and veil before elders they have never met; Muslim women may come into the home of known relatives, before whom they have never veiled. Educated urban families throughout South Asia often disregard these norms and establish new rules more closely related to class and wealth, but the traditional norms remain very powerful. Parents of young women as well as young men retain a large share of control over the choice of a marriage partner in many instances, even among highly educated urban families.

The complexities of purdah observance reveal some of the norms, values, and structures of the wider society but can only be touched on briefly here. There is one major issue, particularly relevant to the family ideology and purdah practices of Muslims, that I want to address separately: the matter of honor.

The Question of Honor

Family status and family honor are inextricably tied up with purdah, as they are throughout the world with matters of women's "being" and "doing," but honor takes on a special salience in many Muslim populations around the globe.

Proverbs express this well: Among the Pathans of northwest Pakistan, for instance, it is said that "A man is known by the qualities of his wife." Another way of putting this (among the Mohmand tribal clans, referred to as Pukhtuns, living along the Afghan border in Pakistan) is that "The Pukhtun's honor is tied to that of his women who exist to serve him and be loyal to his cause. . . . It is a man's world [and] Pukhtuns will not compromise their concept of women. . . . Ideal women learn only to run a household."[9]

Hamida Khala,* an elderly Muslim friend, remembered that in her youth it was a matter of great pride for a man to be able to say "my wife is so pure that no man has seen even the hem

---

*A rough translation of Hamida Khala is "Aunt Hamida." It is a pseudonym.

of her veil." And among the high-status Muslim families who care for an important Muslim saint's shrine in the Delhi area, women told the anthropologist Patricia Jeffery that "the men like purdah because of *izzat* (honor)." She concluded that the seclusion of women was important to the men's work as keepers of the shrine because it showed that they were highly observant, strict Muslims.[10]

The theme of honor, often coupled with the concept of shame, runs through the moral ideas of many societies, particularly around the Mediterranean Sea (western Asia, northern Africa), and is also found in southern Asia in connection with purdah. It is a powerful concept that has been extensively discussed in anthropological studies—but almost always from the male perspective.

In her study of Bedouins, the anthropologist Lila Abu-Lughod offers sensitive new insights into this issue. She traces the relationships among veiling, modesty, and sexuality in a society—unlike many in South Asia—where independent action by men is highly valued, and concludes that: "Separate paths to honor exist, appropriate to the socially and economically independent on the one hand, and to the dependent on the other. . . . The honor of voluntary deference [is] the moral virtue of dependents in Bedouin society."[11]

This point sheds new light on the matter of honor and purdah observance. For instance, one might imagine that making men's honor entirely dependent on women's actions—as in the statements noted earlier—gives women considerable power over men's "derivative" honor. A woman might threaten to ruin a man's reputation by disobedience. But it does not work out that way, for several reasons. First, a man's honor is terribly important to him; in some groups, it is the most cherished attribute, one for which he may be ready to die or to kill. Men have physical and legal power over women: They initiate divorce and can send women back to their families. Depending on the specific type of Islamic personal law in force in a country, women may also be able to initiate divorce; recent legislation in some countries also limits men's power to initiate unilateral divorce. But this is unheard of in those groups where violence is used to defend family honor. Men in such groups often beat women, and, in extreme cases, their concern for personal and family honor may prompt them to kill a female relative who has violated the group's code of conduct. Such killings, like "crimes of passion" elsewhere, are condoned by the community.[12] Second, women themselves may be imbued with the code of honor. Among the Pukhtuns studied by the anthropologist Akbar Ahmed, women are "paradoxically the most fanatic supporters" of the Pukhtun Code. Ahmed reports a couplet in which a woman exhorts a male to uphold the Code at the cost of his life and her happiness.[13]

Although these ideas and actions sound paradoxical, the explanations for them are not difficult, especially in view of Abu-Lughod's analysis. Respect in the community is vital to the family's status and, in all societies, has both symbolic and material implications. Since women are entirely dependent on the family for survival, especially where the rules of purdah limit labor force participation, their own interests demand that they do what they can to advance the collective interests of the family. Strict purdah observance, in addition, is a way for women to gain respect from others in the family and community, as obedience and conformity are highly valued in these societies.

Most critical to the concept of honor, however, are the implications for hierarchical relationships in family and society. The classic posture of deference to a superior not only assures relative safety for the inferior partner but also offers the only available claim for excellence within the hierarchical system. Seen from this perspective, the issue of honor provides men with extraordinary power to control female behavior, precisely because men are passionately concerned with safeguarding their "derivative" honor. Far from giving women any power to affect male behavior, honor becomes a burden, a harness with which to bridle women. Men's passion to preserve their honor—often equated with manliness—becomes a passion to control women. This is the passion that can break out into acts of violence, as when men feel their personal honor threatened by the actions of women. In another sense, the passion to control women breaks out into other kinds of violence against women—as when writers and leaders of social or political movements invoke the fear of sexual anarchy in a whole society as justification for the imposition of purdah and other constraints on women. The apparently voluntary nature of purdah observance must always be examined in terms of the choices open to women in a given situation. Voluntary deference to superiors may well be the moral virtue of dependents and may represent the best available choice, but it indicates a society in which women are kept tightly within bounds and grievously punished for nonconformity.

Encounter with Purdah

It is hard to imagine what it might be like to live in purdah. There are the physical constraints—covering one's face and body some of the time, avoiding certain men all of the time, staying in certain places, and so on—but these are rules that can be taught and learned. What is much harder to imagine is how women learn (and teach) the feelings that make it seem right to do these things. And that, of course, is the question one has to ask about any code of conduct, in any family or group or society.

This question has haunted me for some time, but it took a while for it to float to the surface. When I first met veiled women in the streets of Karachi, Pakistan, in the 1950s, I was very angry. "How dare THEY do this to women?" I thought, not stopping to think, in my anger, just who THEY might be or how the women themselves felt about it.

In those days, a few years after independence from British colonial rule and the partition of India and Pakistan (in 1947), I spent a lot of time in the poorer sections of the city, near the big old markets and the port, getting to know the place and deciding how I was going to do my dissertation research. At that time, it didn't occur to me to do research on purdah; the study of women was not yet an acknowledged part of social science, especially at Harvard, where I was a graduate student. I hadn't yet learned to listen to myself, to hear what most interested me in a place that I found fascinating.

Purdah: Lots of women on the streets in that part of town, but most of them encased in a billowing cloak, the burqa, black or white, that covered a woman entirely, including her face. The women moved in twos or threes usually, sometimes with a man, often with children. Crossing the busy streets, they were hesitant, sometimes lifting a corner of the face veil to peer at the traffic. There was something about these women that bothered me very much and contributed to my anger: I couldn't make eye contact with them! I hadn't realized how much that meant to me, even with strangers, but it did and it still does—that fleeting glimpse, the guessing about another's thoughts and feelings, the recognition when eyes catch and hold. And with these women, it was impossible.

They could see me, if not very clearly, through their veils (on the black burqa) or the eyeholes (on the more traditional white garment), but I could not see them. As far as I was concerned, that made them invisible, because there was no possibility of interaction—and that was, of course, the point. The wearing of the garment signaled to everyone to stay away. I did not know what it meant to the women, to their sense of self, their self-esteem.

I began to think about what it would mean to live like that, what kind of a society would make people need this particular way of hiding from one another. Purdah became a kind of prism: a window into a society that worked only when you turned it to get the best angle but that yielded many new images once you tried it. Analogies to purdah came to mind, but none really fit. On the streets, I couldn't communicate with people inside cars either—but cars were fast and powerful which these women were not. I thought about nuns (in those days all nuns wore habits) but that analogy wasn't right either, even if the costumes had some striking similarities. Nuns announce to the world, by their habits, that they are not sexual beings but "brides of Christ." Pardanashin were signaling something quite different. In a way, their burqas announced openly that they were sexual beings, for very little girls and very old women did not wear the garment, even in families where other females did. I toyed with the interpretation that the burqa so emphasized women's sexuality—by trying to hide it—that all other human qualities were obliterated. Certainly any sense of individuality was erased, at least in public, by the covering of faces. So these crowds of "invisible" women I saw on the streets of Karachi seemed to be women-in-general rather than specific individuals, and I knew nothing about what they thought and felt.

Over the years, I spent time thinking and reading more about purdah, eventually putting these ideas into print. In the late 1970s, an elderly Muslim woman whom I had known for a long time volunteered to tell me about her life. She had grown up in strict purdah, had been married very young, and had finally given up purdah under the strong and persistent pressure of her husband, a civil servant. We talked about her life (and mine) for many days. From her, I began to learn what it had been like to live in purdah.

Purdah and Muslim Identity: The Story of Hamida Khala

She was the youngest in a very large Muslim family in north India. Her mother died when she was three; her father, a highly educated man, held a post at Aligarh University. Hamida Khala remembered a quite happy childhood. Her father was strict but reasonable; his understanding of Islam emphasized living according to the prescriptions of the Quran, and he did not allow superstitions, such as the wearing of amulets, in his family. Purdah was an important part of his beliefs, and Hamida Khala remembered that she longed to put on the burqa because that would mean she had grown up. Her father wanted all his children, both boys and girls, to be well educated; daily lessons were supervised by adult members of the family. The young Hamida was very close to her father and recalled how she had wanted to please him by being obedient.

Her father remarried but Hamida's elder sisters, who had brought her up after their mother's death, did not get along with the new wife. Perhaps that is one reason why the family accepted a marriage proposal for Hamida—then only thirteen, much younger than her sisters had been when they had married. The prospective bridegroom was a widower, much older than Hamida, but known to the family and with a promising job in the civil service. He was said by some relatives to be "modern," and there were rumors that he would stop Hamida from observing purdah. She came to her first adult decision: If he asked her to leave purdah, she would return to her family. After that, she felt more confident and consented to the marriage.

As was customary she did not live with her new husband for a couple of years, until she was about fifteen. His job took them to Calcutta, thousands of miles from her family, and to a small apartment instead of the large house with an open courtyard she had been used to. The trip to Calcutta, by train, was a nightmare: She heard the voices of men all around her and found it hard to walk in her burqa, even though her husband was beside her. She remembered: "I felt helpless, I could do nothing. . . . I wondered will I really have to take off my burqa? He is a man and he will want me to do whatever he wants." In their new home, she found that the servant her husband had hired was a man (no female servants were to be had). She refused to meet him face to face, true to her training, creating serious problems in running the house. Hamida felt increasing pressure to accommodate her husband's wishes and yet remain true to her father's early training.

As a civil servant in colonial India, her husband worked with British, Hindu, and Muslim colleagues. In this sector of colonial society, social life was organized around couples. A married man whose wife could not participate in tea parties and dinners—because she was in purdah—was at a serious disadvantage because social life and work were closely connected. As long as Hamida's husband had been a bachelor, he was invited freely, but once he was married, his colleagues resented the invisibility of his wife. In the recollections of former British colonial residents, this theme comes up repeatedly—"The greatest social stumbling block between the British and the Indians was purdah"—because Indian men would be able to mix socially with British wives while their own wives could not mix with the British.[14] Whether this curious notion of reciprocity was realistic or simply an excuse for racist snobbery, Hamida's husband was clearly affected by these circumstances. She tried to accommodate him by visiting the wives of friends and going for walks with him in her burqa.

The climax of the young Hamida's struggles over remaining in purdah came unexpectedly, at a dinner party in the home of friends where she had visited before. With great emotion, she recalled this event more than forty years later:

They were trying very hard, my husband's friends . . . that somehow or the other I should come out of purdah. A friend had arranged a dinner. His wife was not in purdah but, because of me, women were arranged to sit separately. The men were always in another room. [On this occasion], the time came when we were supposed to go in to dinner. All the women went into the dining hall. They were told to sit leaving one chair empty in between. I thought they were probably expecting some more women. . . . In those times, English times, cards would be put whose seat is for whom, so we sat in the seat with our name. . . .

Suddenly, the men came into the room. They sat in all those empty chairs. What I experienced, I just can't tell you. There was darkness all around me. I couldn't see anything. I had tears in my eyes. I was sitting with my eyes downcast, I couldn't look up. I tried to look once at my husband but he avoided my eyes. . . .

I don't know when the dinner was over. What I ate I don't remember . . . I was on fire. All my attempts, my endeavors to keep my purdah were over. I felt I was without faith, I had sinned. I had gone in front of so many men, all these friends of my husband. They've seen me. My purdah was broken, my purdah that was my faith.

On the way home, Hamida's husband explained that he had not planned this party, that he was not at fault—"I could never be such a tyrant!" he told her—and asked her to forgive and forget.

"But for a long time," she recalled, "I felt that I had sinned that day. How will God forgive me? Then I realized slowly that I would have to change my life." Hamida decided to write to her father, to tell him about the struggle she was going through, and to ask his advice. He wrote back a long letter, telling her that if her marriage might be endangered, then she had to leave purdah. But he added, as she remembered those many years later, that "this present purdah is not Islamic but our men and women have accepted this kind of purdah."

Her father also told Hamida that there was no purdah in Europe and that European men did not mind. But Indians who want to follow the European example, in this respect, would have difficulties, he told her, cautioning that "our men, it doesn't matter how liberated they think they are, they will not endure it that their wife will talk or be informal with other men. From now on, you should always go out with your husband. Don't meet his friends alone without him and don't be informal with them."

This letter consoled her but she was not fully satisfied. On her own, she started reading about purdah and sought out passages in the Quran and hadith that were about women. At that time, early in her married life and before she was twenty years old, she worked out for herself the rules of modest dress and demeanor that she would follow for the rest of her life. "I realized that if you go out without makeup and if you are not wearing a dress that will attract attention," she recalled, "then you can go out." Hamida started wearing long-sleeved blouses and gave up all her makeup and jewelry. She mixed very little and often did not recognize her husband's friends and colleagues because she kept her eyes down in their presence.

She no longer wore the burqa and went for long walks with her husband, rejoicing in her greater physical agility and strength. She still took the burqa with her on trips, just in case, even though she did not wear it. But on one memorable train journey, her husband angrily threw it out the window and she never had another one made. She learned to manage things like bank accounts and dealt with officials on her own, at her husband's insistence. When he died of a heart attack while some of their seven children were still young, she was able to manage the household. She felt sure she could not have done it if she had stayed in purdah, and pitied pardanashin who were forced by circumstances to try managing on their own.

In retrospect, Hamida Khala recalled that "it was a big sacrifice for me to leave purdah . . . [but my husband] had a lot of respect for me. . . . He knew that it was part of my religion and still I left it. . . . We learned a lot from each other." Her views on purdah could be summed up in three sentences—and there were many people in Pakistan who felt the same way, at least in the 1960s and 70s: "The real purdah is modesty (*haya*). If a woman has no modesty, then even in a burqa she is not in purdah. If she has modesty, she is in purdah even without burqa." But Hamida went further. With evident delight, she recounted that a man from a very conservative group had come to call on her one day, knowing she had been in purdah and was the widow of an important man, to solicit her support for bringing back widespread purdah in Pakistan. He spoke to her of the harm that would be done to the country if women did not wear burqas. She smiled at the memory of what she told him: "Let a thousand women come out at once, not just a few. Then you will see how quickly men get used to seeing women and think nothing of it." She had come out of purdah herself, after all, and had kept her modesty, she added, and that was what mattered.

I do not know whether the life of Hamida Khala is unusual or typical, even for her generation and class. But her story showed me how deeply the values and rules of purdah are embedded in a person's life. Leaving purdah was not as easy as I had perhaps imagined; it was not a matter of throwing off the burqa like an overcoat in spring. Hamida Khala's story of growth and change can be seen as her struggle to define a Muslim identity for herself, at a time when conflicting pressures from past and present, father and husband, made things hard for her.

Famidabi: The Muslim Union Organizer

Perhaps I was wrong: Not all changes were as dramatic or as difficult as Hamida Khala's. In 1985, a friend told me another true story, about Famidabi, an organizer in the Self-Employed Women's Association (SEWA), a trade union of very poor women in India. Famidabi had told the story herself, at a SEWA convention.

Famidabi was the elected head of the SEWA group in Bhopal, organized by the women who earn low piecework wages rolling country cigarettes (bidi). Her home was a couple of rooms in a slum where she lived with her family. As a Muslim, Famidabi observed purdah and wore a burqa, as was customary among Muslims in Bhopal. Being in purdah was probably one reason she worked in a home industry, bidi making. When the invitation came to attend the regional SEWA meeting, Famidabi reluctantly agreed to the request of other union members that she go, but insisted that another woman travel with her.

On the way to the railway station, with her son carrying her bag (as she later told the conference group), some of the women from her union called out to her: "And will you make revolution wearing a burqa?" Famidabi turned around, went home, and came back without the burqa, even though she saw from her son's behavior that he did not approve. She told the conference: "I felt they had chosen me and I should go by their advice" but, looking at her disapproving son from the train window, she had wondered, "Have I done something bad?" She consoled herself by thinking that her son would not be so shocked later, when his wife or daughter also threw away her burqa.

Another woman stood up at the conference and told of her advice to another group of Muslim women bidi workers: "You must leave your purdah! You are not even getting the benefit of minimum wage regulations because you won't go yourselves to deal with the middlemen. You send your children. You deserve to be paid less!"

Famidabi and Hamida Khala stand at almost the opposite ends of the social and economic spectrum, although Famidabi is not among the poorest of the poor and Hamida Khala not among the wealthy or the most sophisticated. Their stories show how purdah functions at these different points in society and, of course, in time. Famidabi acted in the 1980s, and most of Hamida Khala's struggles came in the 1920s and 1930s. For Hamida Khala, earning an income from a job was neither an option nor a necessity; for Famidabi it was both. In both cases, purdah observance was tied up with religious feelings and with the respect accorded by others in the community, but the actions the two women were able to take reflected the differences in their circumstances.

Projections of Purdah: Implications for Social Order

Rokeya Sakhawat Hossain was not the first writer to describe purdah in South Asia nor the first to oppose it, but I know of none to equal the ferocity of her accounts and of only a few who also translated their concern into action. For the most part, of those who have written about purdah, "outsider" accounts tend to be critical and the "insiders" to adopt a moralistic tone. For non-Asian observers, purdah is usually as unique as it was for me, and it colors other perceptions of Asia. For those who have grown up in purdah-observing environments, it is often so unremarkable as to remain unmentioned except by moralists.

In the early nineteenth century, an Englishwoman married to an Indian Muslim of high status wrote one of the earliest accounts of life in urban zenanas, to which she had access through her husband's family connections.[15] She was clearly fascinated by meeting women in seclusion but enjoyed her conversations with men more, especially those about comparative religion. Her attitude toward the women was one of kindly condescension and she was a bit ambivalent about Indian customs, although much more tolerant than many English residents who came to India later. Mrs. Meer Hassan Ali's accounts make it possible to trace some of the changes and similarities in purdah practices in north India: For example, she makes no mention of anyone wearing a burqa or even knowing about it. This supports a view of purdah as an unstable institution.

Nearly a century later, a very different account of purdah was written by another foreign observer. Katherine Mayo had an overriding political purpose: to ridicule Indian aspirations for national independence by writing a sensational account purportedly "exposing" issues relating to women, family life, sexuality, and seclusion. Her highly moralistic account focuses on purdah—which she calls "life imprisonment within the four walls of the home"—and early marriage. In a typical passage, she writes that Indians suffered from "undeniable race deterioration" brought on by "sexual indulgence," which made "their hands . . . too weak, too fluttering to seize or hold the reins of Government" at the age when "the Anglo-Saxon is just coming into full glory of manhood."[16] Although Mayo's account has been praised by modern feminist writers,[17] her obvious political purposes and her racism make her a very unreliable witness. The tone of Mayo's book on Indian society is remarkably similar, however, to some equally moralistic accounts of other societies by those South Asians who urged that purdah must be retained to prevent moral chaos.

One of the most prominent Muslim writers to support purdah was Abul A'la Maududi, whose works have achieved wide circulation not only in South Asia but in many other parts of the world. Maududi's work on purdah first appeared in 1939; an English version was published in Pakistan in 1972 as *Purdah and the Status of Woman in Islam*.

Maududi's dualistic view of humanity is expressed as follows: "All actions that take place in the world cannot take place unless there exists a passive partner for every active partner, and the passive partner possesses the qualities of yielding and surrendering." The imagery of the male as cultivator and the female as his field is common among Muslims and recurs often in Maududi's books. And although, like many other writers of hortative works, he takes the position that he is merely writing obvious common sense with which no reasonable person could possibly disagree, Maududi does add the following disclaimer: " 'Activity' in itself is naturally superior to 'passivity' and femininity. This superiority is not due to any merit in masculinity against any demerit in femininity."[18]

If such statements sound familiar to Western readers, it is because the same type of dualism has been deeply embedded in the Judeo-Christian tradition since its earliest days. In the terms I have used in this essay, claims for women's "special" nature also reflect the dualistic philosophical tradition; they are directly relevant to the contemporary challenges presented by revivalist movements that stress a dualistic view of women and men.

Feminist theologians have been critical of the dualistic tradition in the Judeo-Christian heritage for some time. According to Rosemary Ruether's analysis, for example, St. Augustine equated the dualism of body and soul with the dualism of male and female: "Thus the spiritual image of God . . . in man became essentially male and femaleness was equated with the lower, corporeal nature."[19] More recent arguments have been advanced with respect to the same kind of dualism within Islam. The Muslim feminist theologian Riffat Hassan argues that dualism found its way into Islam from the Judeo-Christian tradition by way of the commentaries on the Quran, even though this type of dualism appears to be alien to the Quran itself. Hassan also notes that the woman's "body" is seen as her "essence" through the association of mind/body dualism with male/female distinctions.[20] It is ironic to consider that the dualistic conception may be a legacy from the Judeo-Christian heritage, when it is precisely this heritage from which the new Islamic movements are trying to distance themselves at the present time.

Maududi's views about women did not go unchallenged. For instance, in the early 1970s, a male Pakistani writer devoted a whole book to the analysis of purdah because he was convinced that "the questions of purdah and polygamy are, fundamentally, the questions of hindrances to the progress and development of the Muslim society, civilisation and culture."[21] This view was widely shared at the time, especially in urban areas.

More recently, however, things have changed in a number of countries with large Muslim populations with regard to the position of women. The views of powerful social and political movements have influenced a number of governments to enforce policies that ensure the support of these movements at the expense of women. To take Pakistan as an example—although it is by no means the only country where this has happened—government directives made it clear beginning in 1980 that rights previously taken for granted would now be sharply limited or even withdrawn altogether. It began with orders to government employees to wear "Islamic dress" at work; this also applied to educational institutions. These directives were widely disregarded, but they encouraged "the more zealous to implement their subjective code of dress on women" whom they saw in public places. The policies were, at first, presented in terms of encouraging people to follow their own cultural norms and reject Western patterns, but critics soon argued that women were forced "to adhere to codes of conduct and dress which for men are considered antiquated, and of placing restrictions on the female half of the population exclusively."[22] In short, the revival of purdah norms was the beginning of widespread attempts to limit the rights of women and enforce the segregation of women and men. Women responded with protests and demonstrations organized by both existing and newly mobilized groups, but they were unable to prevent the enactment of legislation that sharply limited women's legal rights.

Sexuality and the Fear of Social Chaos

Proponents of purdah are often explicit in their fears of the consequences of sexual attraction between women and men. They insist that only the most stringent controls over male-female interaction will preserve a society from what they see as moral chaos. As stated by Maududi: "Sexual attraction which naturally exists between the sexes as a strong instinctive urge becomes all too powerful, even rebellious, to transgress all limits with every impetus it receives from the free intermingling of the men and women." In support of stringent sex segregation, proponents of purdah often recount examples of unusual sexual practices, prostitution, divorce, and pornography in Western countries. These accounts are taken from newspapers and magazines, particularly those with large international circulations, and are described as typical of everyday life. Maududi, whose works are important to note because they have been widely distributed, cites many such accounts, especially in writing of the "national suicide" of Western countries (especially France, England, and the United States), which he attributes to "the logical consequences of the movement which was initiated in the beginning of the 19th century for the rights and emancipation of women."[23]

Similar calls for a return to the "good old days" when they imagine social controls were strict is also common among fundamentalists in the Judeo-Christian tradition, but a preoccupation with sexuality among Muslims may need to be seen from another angle as well. According to some recent Muslim feminist writers, the association between sexual attraction and female passivity raises important questions about women and men in Muslim societies. "Why are silence, immobility, and obedience the key criteria of female beauty in the Muslim society where I live and work?" asks Fatna Sabbah, the pseudonymous author, a Muslim woman, of *Woman in the Muslim Unconscious.* "Why, according to the canons of beauty in Islamic literature, does a woman who does not express herself excite desire in a man?"[24] Although this is a large and controversial issue that needs more careful discussion among Muslims than it has so far received, a peculiarly appropriate comment on Sabbah's questions comes from Lila Abu-Lughod's interpretation of honor and veiling among Egyptian Bedouins: "Sexuality is the most potent threat to the patrilineal, patricentered system and to the authority of those who uphold it . . . and women are those most closely identified with sexuality through their reproductive activities. Therefore, to show respect for that social order and the people who represent it, women must deny their sexuality. They do so by denying sexual interests—avoiding and acting uninterested in men, dressing modestly so as not to draw attention to their sexual charms, and veiling." This interpretation is consis-

tent with the same author's depiction of "the honor of voluntary deference" as the "moral virtue of dependents,"[25] which I
discussed earlier. Stated in the terms used in that society, these
are the ideas that underlie and reinforce the view of sexuality
as a source of anarchy in an otherwise ordered society, an anarchy that lies close enough to the surface to require constant
watchfulness and control.

Beyond the psychological and symbolic significance of these
concepts of women and sexuality, there is also the concrete
material base of patrilineal, patriarchal societies that deeply af-
fects both sexuality and reproduction. Among Muslims, for example, the legitimacy of children is of major importance in
preserving a sense of order in the society and controlling the
inheritance of property. Legitimacy is a major issue in Muslim
personal law, particularly in connection with the regulation of
marriage and divorce and in the inheritance of property. Sexuality poses a concrete threat to the social order because mutual
attraction may upset careful parental plans for a future marriage
alliance. Since women can legally inherit property under Muslim personal law (even if they do not always receive what they
are entitled to), the property inherited by a daughter can po-
tentially leave the control of the patrilineage. This is one factor
in the preference for marriage arrangements with paternal kin,
especially between the children of brothers who may jointly
control family property. Sexuality, in short, has a legitimate
place only in family life.

Purdah and the Natural Rights of Women

At the end, I return to the beginning, to Rokeya's message to
her readers to wake up to their self-interests and to regain their
natural rights. To my mind, this is the real significance of her
story and of all her later work. Purdah must be seen, as I think
she saw it, not simply as a matter of veiling or not veiling
female faces but as a way of putting half the population at a
disadvantage in dealing with the world.

In "Sultana's Dream" Rokeya stood purdah on its head,
shocking her readers and revealing, through "reverse purdah,"
many of the implications of sex segregation. Reverse purdah
was at least imaginable to Rokeya's readers, in ways that a world

completely without men (like Charlotte Perkins Gilman's *Herland*[26]) or an egalitarian world might not have been. Rokeya was not as explicit as she might have been about the cruel consequences of confinement for the men of Ladyland, concentrating attention instead on what life in Ladyland meant to previously confined women.

Beyond its shock value, Rokeya's story directly challenges the ideas by which her readers had been taught to live in family and society. This challenge took two main forms: a call for women to reconsider their self-interest and a demonstration of women's competence in the world outside the home.

The concept of self-interest that was instilled in South Asian women in Rokeya's time—and that still prevails today among many people—is not that of an independent individual but of a member of the family, whose collective interests determine the actions of individuals. In this view, there is very little room for the "natural rights" that Rokeya may have had in mind in "Sultana's Dream." Where women's interests are so tightly bound up with the interests of the family, it is hard to imagine a woman acting against family interests.

But Rokeya, the rebel and reformer, was also a product of this environment, and who can say whether there were not others like her? The life histories women tell these days about their mothers and grandmothers and aunts suggest that streams of resentment and muted rebellion run deep in some unexpected places. If there were other Rokeyas, we will perhaps learn about them from the life histories now being talked about and written down all over South Asia. And they will be worth waiting for.

Notes to Afterword

1. Meredith Borthwick, *The Changing Role of Women in Bengal, 1849–1905* (Princeton, N.J.: Princeton University Press, 1984), is one of several authors making this point with specific reference to women's position. See also Dagmar Engels, "The Limits of Gender Ideology: Bengali Women, the Colonial State, and the Private Sphere, 1890–1930," Paper presented at the Seventh Berkshire Conference on the History of Women, Wellesley College, June 19–21, 1987.

2. John T. Platts, *A Dictionary of Urdu, Classical Hindi and English* (Oxford: Oxford University Press, 1960), pp. 246–47.

3. More details on purdah observance and the analysis of purdah practices can be found in many sources, as indicated in Carol Sakala's comprehensive, annotated bibliography, *Women of South Asia: A Guide to Resources* (Millwood, N.Y.: Kraus International Publications, 1980). A collection of articles about purdah, by both U.S. and South Asian authors, appears in Hanna Papanek and Gail Minault, eds., *Separate Worlds: Studies of Purdah in South Asia* (Columbia, Mo.: South Asia Books, and Delhi: Chanakya Publishers, 1982). Another source on Muslim purdah is Patricia Jeffery, *Frogs in a Well: Indian Women in Purdah* (London: Zed Press, 1979). On Hindu purdah, see Ursula Sharma, "Women and Their Affines: The Veil as a Symbol of Separation," *Man (N.S.)* 13, no. 2 (June 1978): 218–33, and *Women, Work and Property in North-West India* (London: Tavistock Publications, 1980). Detailed descriptions of purdah in a very conservative Hindu household appear in a novel by Rama Mehta, *Inside the Haveli* (New Delhi: Arnold-Heinemann Publishers, 1977), also excerpted in Papanek and Minault.

4. See, for example, Papanek and Minault, eds., *Separate Worlds*, p. 23.

5. See especially Sylvia Vatuk, "Purdah Revisited: A Comparison of Hindu and Muslim Interpretations of the Cultural Meaning of Purdah in South Asia," in ibid., pp. 54–78.

6. Jeffery, *Frogs in a Well*.

7. Sharma, "Women and Their Affines," p. 226.

8. Lila Abu-Lughod, *Veiled Sentiments: Honor and Poetry in a Bedouin Society* (Berkeley: University of California Press, 1986), pp. 56–57.

9. Akbar S. Ahmed, *Pakistan Society: Islam, Ethnicity and Leadership in South Asia* (Karachi: Oxford University Press, 1986), p. 29.

10. Jeffery, *Frogs in a Well*, p. 165.

11. Abu-Lughod, *Veiled Sentiments*, p. 165.

12. For recent examples, see Akbar S. Ahmed, *Pakistan Society*, pp. 32–33.

13. Ibid., pp. 29–30.

14. Charles Allen, ed., *Plain Tales from the Raj* (London: Andre Deutsch Ltd., 1975), p. 235.

15. Mrs. Meer Hassan Ali, *Observations on the Mussulmauns of India: Descriptive of Their Manners, Customs, Habits and Religious Opinions, made during a Twelve Years' Residence in their immediate Society*, 2 vols. (London: Parbury, Allen and Co., 1832). Second ed., edited with notes and a biographical introduction by W. Crooke, appeared in 1917 and was reprinted in India (Delhi: Deep Publications, 1975).

16. Katherine Mayo, *Mother India* (New York: Harcourt, Brace & Co., 1927), pp. 111, 32.

17. Mary Daly, *Gyn/Ecology: The Metaethics of Radical Feminism* (Boston: Beacon Press, 1978), pp. 119–22, 127–29, 438–39.

18. S. Abul A'la Maududi, *Purdah and the Status of Woman in Islam*, trans. and ed. Al-Ash'ari (Lahore: Islamic Publications Ltd., 1972), p. 37.

19. Rosemary Radford Ruether, *Liberation Theology* (New York: Paulist Press, 1972), p. 99.

20. Riffat Hassan, "Equal Before Allah?: Woman–Man Equality in the Islamic Tradition," *Harvard Divinity Bulletin* 17, no. 2 (Jan.–May 1987): 2–4. See also Hassan, "Women in the Context of Change and Confrontation within Muslim Communities," in *Women of Faith in Dialogue*, ed. Virginia Ramey Mollenkott (New York: Crossroad Publishing Company, 1987), pp. 96–109.

21. Mazhar ul Haq Khan, *Purdah and Polygamy: A Study in the Social Pathology of the Muslim Society* (Peshawar: Nashiran-e-Ilm-o-Taraqiyet, 1972), p. 1.

22. Khawar Mumtaz and Farida Shaheed, eds., *Women of Pakistan: Two Steps Forward, One Step Back?* (London: Zed Books Ltd., 1987), pp. 78–79.

23. S. Abul A'la Maududi, *Purdah and the Status of Woman*, p. 59.

24. Fatna A. Sabbah, *Woman in the Muslim Unconscious* (New York: Pergamon Press, 1984), p. 3.

25. Abu-Lughod, *Veiled Sentiments*, p. 165.

26. Charlotte Perkins Gilman, *Herland* (New York: Pantheon Books, 1979).

Glossary

Ammajan	Mother
Anchal	The end of a sari
Apajan	Older sister
Ayah	Maidservant, particularly one taking care of children
Begum	(Turkish) The wife of a Beg, a titled nobleman; by extension, a Muslim gentlewoman; analogous to *Madame* or *Signora*
Brahmo	A member of Brahmo Samaj, a movement founded by Ram Mohan Roy in 1828 to encourage modernization and female education; not to be confused with Brahmin, the highest caste classification in Hindu society
Burqa	An all-enveloping tentlike cloak worn by some Muslim women in public in South Asia
Dada	Older brother
Gurkha	A Nepali ethnic group, many members of which served in the British army, now also in the Indian army
Hadith	Religious tradition based on the sayings of the Prophet
Jihad	Holy war
Mardana	Men's quarters where they receive guests; outer rooms or apartments; compare with *zenana*
Motichur	A type of candy popular in Bengal and Bihar and in present-day Bangladesh
Muni	A Hindu religious seer and lawgiver

Puthi	A popular tale written in verse
Teapoy	A small, three-legged table for serving tea
Zemindar	A large landowner
Zenana	Women's living quarters; note that men sleep and often eat in the women's part of the house; by extension, secluded women

Publications of
Rokeya Sakhawat Hossain

Motichur, Part 1. Gurudas Chattopadhyaya & Sons, 201 Corn-wallis Street, Calcutta. 1908. A collection of articles published from 1903–4 in various journals.

Sultana's Dream. S. K. Lahiri & Co., College Street, Calcutta. 1908. Originally published in *The Indian Ladies' Magazine*, Madras, 1905.

Motichur, Part 2. Mrs. R. S. Hossain (publisher), Calcutta. 1921. Dedicated to Apajan Karimunessa Khanam.

Padmaraga (Ruby). Mrs. R. S. Hossain (publisher), Calcutta. 1924. Dedicated to Dada Abul Asad Mohammed Ibrahim Saber.

Avarodhbasini (The Secluded Ones). Mohammadi Book Agency, 29 Upper Circular Road, Calcutta. 1928. Dedicated to Ammajan Rahatunnessa Sabera Chowdhurani. Also appeared as a series of columns in the *Monthly Mohammadi*, 1928–29.

Rokeya Racanavali (Collected Works of Rokeya), edited by Abdul Quadir. The Bangla Academy, Dhaka. 1973.

The Feminist Press at the City University of New York is a nonprofit literary and educational institution dedicated to publishing work by and about women. Our existence is grounded in the knowledge that women's writing has often been absent or underrepresented on bookstore and library shelves and in educational curricula—and that such absences contribute, in turn, to the exclusion of women from the literary canon, from the historical record, and from the public discourse.

The Feminist Press was founded in 1970. In its early decades, the Feminist Press launched the contemporary rediscovery of "lost" American women writers, and went on to diversify its list by publishing significant works by American women writers of color. More recently, the Press's publishing program has focused on international women writers, who remain far less likely to be translated than male writers, and on nonfiction works that explore issues affecting the lives of women around the world.

Founded in an activist spirit, the Feminist Press is currently undertaking initiatives that will bring its books and educational resources to under-served populations, including community colleges, public high schools and middle schools, literacy and ESL programs, and prison education programs. As we move forward into the twenty-first century, we continue to expand our work to respond to women's silences wherever they are found.

Many of our readers support the Press with their memberships, which are tax-deductible. Members receive numerous benefits, including complimentary publications, discounts on all purchases from our catalog or web site, pre-publication notification of new books and notice of special sales, invitations to special events, and a subscription to our email newsletter, "Women's Words: News from the Feminist Press."

For more information about membership and events, and for a complete catalog of the Press's 250 books, please refer to our web site: www.feministpress.org.